Also by
Lucy & Stephen Hawking

GEORGE'S SECRET KEY
TO THE UNIVERSE

GEORGE'S COSMIC
TREASURE HUNT

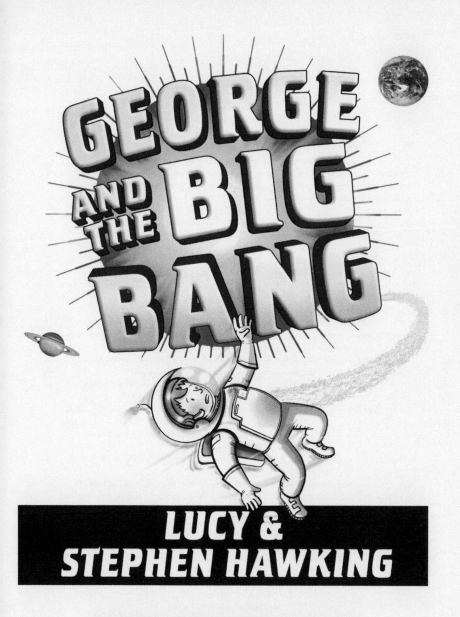

GEORGE AND THE BIG BANG

LUCY & STEPHEN HAWKING

ILLUSTRATED BY GARRY PARSONS

Simon & Schuster Books for Young Readers
New York   London   Toronto   Sydney   New Delhi

SIMON & SCHUSTER BOOKS FOR YOUNG READERS
An imprint of Simon & Schuster Children's Publishing Division
1230 Avenue of the Americas, New York, New York 10020

Text copyright © 2011 by Lucy Hawking
Illustrations by Garry Parsons
Illustrations/diagrams copyright © 2011 by Random House Children's Books
Originally published in Great Britain in 2011 by Doubleday
First U.S. Edition 2012

The Library of Congress has catalogued the hardcover edition as follows:
Hawking, Lucy.
George and the big bang / Lucy & Stephen Hawking ; illustrated by Garry Parsons. — 1st U.S. ed.
p. cm.
Summary: George tries to escape a host of problems by going to Switzerland to
help his friend Annie's father, Eric, run an experiment exploring the origins of the universe,
but faces saboteurs and a mysterious message from George's old nemesis, Reeper, there.
Includes scientific essays exploring the latest theories on the origin of the universe.
ISBN 978-1-4424-4005-0 (hc)
[1. Science—Experiments—Fiction. 2. Big Bang theory—Fiction. 3. Sabotage—Fiction.
4. Switzerland—Fiction.] I. Hawking, S. W. (Stephen W.) II. Parsons, Garry, ill. III. Title.
PZ7.H3134Gc 2012
[Fic]—dc23
2011035361
ISBN 978-1-4424-4006-7 (pbk)
ISBN 978-1-4424-4007-4 (eBook)

For Willa, Lola and George,
Rose, George, William and Charlotte

THE LATEST SCIENTIFIC THEORIES!

Within the story are a number of terrific essays on scientific topics that give readers real insight into some of the latest theories. These have been written by the following eminent scientists:

SPECIFIC FACTUAL SECTIONS

There is lots of science within this book, but there are also a number of separate sections where facts and information are provided on specific subjects. Some readers may wish to refer to these pages in particular.

Chapter One

Where's the best place in the Universe for a pig to live? Annie was typing onto the keyboard of Cosmos, the supercomputer. "Cosmos will know!" she declared. "He must be able to find Freddy somewhere better than that shabby old farm."

The farm where Freddy, the pig, now lived was actually perfectly nice—at least, all the other animals seemed happy there. Only Freddy, George's precious pig, was miserable.

"I feel awful," said George sadly as Cosmos, the world's greatest supercomputer, ran through his millions and billions of files to try to answer Annie's question about pigs. "Freddy was so angry he wouldn't even look at me."

"He looked at *me*!" said Annie hotly, glaring at the screen. "I definitely saw him send me a message with his piggy eyes.

1

It was: *HELP! GET ME OUT OF HERE!"*

The day trip to visit Freddy at the farm just outside Foxbridge, the university town where George and Annie lived, had not been a success. When Annie's mom, Susan, arrived to pick them up at the end of the afternoon, she was surprised to see George red-faced and furious and Annie on the verge of tears.

"George! Annie!" said Susan. "What is the matter with the two of you?"

"It's Freddy!" burst out Annie, leaping into the backseat of the car. "He hates it at the farm."

Freddy was George's pet pig. He had been a Christmas present from George's gran when he was a piglet. George's parents were eco-activists, which also meant they weren't very interested in presents. They didn't like the way all the discarded, broken, and unwanted toys left over from Christmas built up into huge mounds of old plastic and metal, floating across the seas, choking whales and strangling seagulls, or making mountains of ugly junk on the land.

George's gran knew that if she gave George an ordinary present, his parents would give it right back, and everyone would get upset. So if he was to keep his Christmas present, she realized she would have to think of something special — something that *helped* the planet rather than destroyed it.

That's why, one cold Christmas Eve, George found a cardboard box on the doorstep. Inside it was a little pink piglet and a note from Gran saying: *Can you give this young pig a nice home?* George had been thrilled. He had a Christmas present his parents had to let him keep; and, even better, he had his very own pig.

The problem with little pink piglets, however, is that they get bigger. Bigger and bigger, until they are enormous—too large for the backyard of an ordinary row house with a narrow strip of land and scattered vegetables growing between the two fences separating it from the neighboring yards. But George's parents had kind hearts really, so Freddy, as George named the pig, had continued living in his pigsty in the backyard until he reached a gigantic size—he was now more like a baby elephant than a pig. George didn't care how big Freddy got—he was very fond of his pig and spent long hours in the yard, chatting to him or just sitting in his huge shadow, reading books about the wonders of the cosmos.

But George's dad, Terence, had never really liked

Freddy. Freddy was too big, too piggy, too pink, and he enjoyed dancing on Terence's carefully arranged vegetable plot, trampling his spinach and broccoli and munching thoughtlessly on his carrot tops. Last summer, before the twins were born, the whole family had been going away. Terence had been super-quick to find Freddy a place at a nearby children's petting farm, promising George that when they all got back, the pig would be able to come home.

Only this never happened. George and his parents returned from their adventures, and George's next-door neighbors—the scientist Eric, his wife, Susan, and their daughter, Annie—came back from living in America. Then George's mother had twin baby girls, Juno and Hera, who cried and gurgled and smiled. And then cried some more. And every time one of them stopped crying, there would be a beautiful half-second of silence. Then the other baby would start up, wailing until George thought his brain would explode and start leaking out of his ears. His mom and dad always looked stressed and tired, and George felt bad about asking them for anything at all. So once Annie came back from America, he started slipping through the hole in the back fence more and more often, until he was practically living with his friend, her crazy family, and the world's greatest supercomputer in the house next door.

But it was worse for Freddy, because he never made it home at all.

Once the baby girls were born, George's dad said they had enough on their hands without a great big pig taking up most of the backyard. "Anyway," he told George rather pompously when he protested, "Freddy is a creature of planet Earth. He doesn't belong to you—he belongs to nature."

But Freddy couldn't even stay in his small, friendly petting farm, which had to close at the beginning of this summer vacation. Freddy—along with the other animals there—had been moved to a bigger place where there were unusual breeds of farm animal, and lots of visitors, especially during summer vacation. It was a bit like him and Annie moving up to middle school, George thought to himself—going somewhere much bigger. It was a bit scary.

"Nature, huh!" he snorted to himself as he remembered his dad's comments now. Cosmos the computer was still chewing over the complicated question of the best location in the Universe for a homeless pig. "I don't think Freddy knows he's a creature of planet Earth—he just wants to be with us," said George.

"He looked so sad!" said Annie. "I'm sure he was crying."

On their trip to the farm earlier that day, George and Annie had come across Freddy lying flat on his stomach on the floor of his pig pen, legs splayed out on either side, his eyes dull and his cheeks sunken. The other pigs were trotting around, looking cheerful and

healthy. The pen was spacious and airy, the farm clean, and the people that worked there friendly. But even so, Freddy seemed lost in a piggy hell of his own. George felt incredibly guilty. Summer vacation had passed and he hadn't done anything about getting Freddy home again. It was Annie who had suggested making the trip to the farm today, badgering her mom into driving them there and picking them up again afterward.

George and Annie had asked the workers what was wrong with Freddy. They'd looked worried too. The vet had examined him: Freddy wasn't sick, she'd said; he just seemed very unhappy, as though he was pining away. After all, he had grown up in George's quiet backyard, and had then moved to a small farm with just a few children coming to pet him. In the new place he was surrounded by noisy, unfamiliar animals and had lots of visitors every day: It was probably a big shock. Freddy had never lived with his fellow pigs before. He was totally unused to other animals: In fact, he considered himself more as a person than a pig. He didn't understand what he was doing on a farm where visitors hung over the edge of the pig pen to stare at him.

"Can't we take him home?" George had asked.

The helpers looked a little perplexed. There were lots of rules and regulations about moving animals around, and anyway, they felt that Freddy was simply too big now to live in an urban backyard. "He'll feel better soon!" they reassured George. "Just you wait and see— next time you come to visit, it'll be quite different."

"But he's been here for weeks already," protested George.

The helpers either didn't hear or chose to ignore him.

Annie, however, had other ideas. As soon as they got back to her house, she started making plans. "We can't bring Freddy back to your place," she said, switching on Cosmos, "because your dad will just take him straight back to the farm. And he can't live here with us."

Unfortunately George knew this was true. He looked around Eric's study: Cosmos was perched on the desk, on top of piles and piles of scientific papers, surrounded by wobbling towers of books, cups of half-drunk tea, and scraps of paper with important equations scrawled

7

on them. Annie's dad used the supercomputer to work on his theories about the origins of the Universe. Finding a home for a pig was, it seemed, almost as difficult.

When Annie and her family had first moved into this house, George's pig had made a dramatic entrance, charging through Eric's study, sending books flying into the air. Eric had been quite pleased, because in all the chaos Freddy had actually helped him to find a book he'd been searching for. But these days, George and Annie both knew that Eric wouldn't welcome a spare pig. He had too much work to do to look after a pig.

"We need to find somewhere nice for Freddy," said Annie firmly.

Ping! Cosmos's screen came to life again and started flashing with different colored lights—a sure sign that the great computer was pleased with himself. "I have prepared for you a summary of the conditions within our local cosmic area and their suitability for porcine life," he said. "Please click on each box to see a readout of your pig's existence on each planet within our Solar System. I have taken the liberty of providing"—the computer chortled to himself—"an illustration for each planet with my own comments."

"Wowzers!" said Annie. "Cosmos, you are the *best*."

On Cosmos's screen were eight little boxes, each marked with the name of a planet in the Solar System. She checked the one labeled MERCURY . . .

Mercury
Scorched pig

Jupiter
Sinking pig

Venus
Smelly pig

Saturn
Orbital pig

Earth
Happy pig

Uranus
Upside-down pig

Mars
Bouncy pig

Neptune
Windy pig

OUR SOLAR SYSTEM

The Solar System is the name we give to the family of planets that orbit our star, the Sun.

How Our Solar System Was Created

Our Solar System was formed around 4.6 billion years ago

 Step One:
A cloud of gas and dust begins to collapse—possibly triggered by shock waves from a nearby supernova.

 Step Two:
A ball of dust formed, spinning round and flattening into a disk as it attracted more dust, gradually growing larger and spinning faster.

 Step Three:
The central region of this collapsed cloud got hotter and hotter until it started to burn, turning it into a star.

Step Four:
As the star burned, the dust in the disk around it slowly stuck together to form clusters, which became rocks, which eventually formed planets, all still orbiting the star—our Sun—at the center. These planets ended up forming two main groups: close to the Sun, where it is hot, the rocky planets; farther out, beyond Mars, the gas planets, which consist of a thick atmosphere of gas surrounding a liquid inner region with, very probably, a solid core.

Stars with a mass like our Sun take around ten million years to form.

Step Five:

The planets cleaned up their orbits by gobbling up any chunks of material they came across.

> Because Jupiter is the largest, it may have done most of the cleaning up itself.

 Step Six:

Hundreds of millions of years later, the planets settled into stable orbits—the same orbits that they follow today. The bits of stuff left over ended up either in the asteroid belt between Mars and Jupiter, or much farther out beyond Pluto in the Kuiper belt.

Are There Other Solar Systems Like Ours?

For several hundred years astronomers suspected that other stars in the Universe might have planets in orbit around them. However, the first exoplanet was not confirmed until 1992, orbiting the corpse of a massive star. The first planet around a real, brightly shining star was discovered in 1995. Since then, more than four hundred exoplanets have been discovered—some around stars very similar to our Sun!

> An exoplanet is a planet in orbit around a star other than the Earth's Sun.

This is just the beginning. Even if only 10% of the stars in our Galaxy had planets in orbit around them, that would still mean more than *two hundred billion solar systems* within the Milky Way alone.

Some of these may be similar to our Solar System. Others might look very different. Planets in a binary solar system, for example, might see two suns rise and set in the sky. Knowing the distance from their star to the planets—and the size and age of the star—helps us to calculate how likely it is that we might find life on those planets.

Most of the exoplanets we know about in other solar systems are huge—as big as Jupiter or larger— mainly because those are easier to detect than smaller planets. But astronomers are beginning to discover smaller, rocky planets orbiting at the right distance from their star that might be more like planet Earth.

In early 2011, NASA confirmed their Kepler mission had spotted an Earth-like planet around a star five hundred light-years away! At only 1.4 times the size of our home planet, this new planet, Kepler 10-b, may be the most similar to Earth we have found so far.

Chapter Two

"But I don't think Freddy could actually live on any of those planets," objected George after they had looked through Cosmos's tour of the Solar System for pigs. "He'd boil on Mercury, get blown away on Neptune, or sink through layers of poisonous gas on Saturn. He'd probably wish he was back on the farm."

"Except for on Earth . . . ," murmured Annie. "That's the only planet in our Solar System that's suitable for life." Her nose was scrunched up, meaning she was thinking hard. "It's just like for humans," she said suddenly. "You know how my dad was talking about finding a new home for human beings, in case our planet becomes uninhabitable?"

"You mean, if we get struck by a huge comet or global warming takes over?" said George. "We won't be able to live on this planet if there are volcanic eruptions or it becomes a huge, dry desert." George knew all about the frightening things that might happen to planet Earth if humans didn't start taking better care of it from his eco-activist parents.

ASTEROID ATTACK!

 An asteroid is a rocky fragment left over from the formation of the Solar System about 4.6 billion years ago. Scientists estimate there are probably millions of asteroids in our Solar System.

Asteroids typically range in size from as little as a few yards to hundreds of miles across.

 Once in a while an asteroid will get nudged out of its orbit—for example by the gravity of nearby planets—possibly sending it on a collision course with the Earth.

 Around once a year, a rock the size of a family car crashes into the Earth's atmosphere but burns up before it reaches the surface.

Once every few thousand years, a chunk of rock about the size of a football field hits the Earth, and every few million years, Earth suffers an impact from a space object—an asteroid or a comet—large enough to threaten civilization.

 If an asteroid or a comet—a rocky ice ball that slingshots around the Sun—were to hit the surface of the Earth, it is possible that it could crash through the surface, releasing a flood of volcanic eruptions. Nothing would survive the impact.

A **meteoroid** is a chunk of rock that flies through our Solar System; a **meteorite** is what you call that piece of rock if it lands on the Earth.

Sixty-five million years ago, an asteroid smashed into the Earth. This could be what wiped out the dinosaurs—the impact sent up a cloud of fine dust, which blocked out the sunlight, dooming the dinosaurs and many other species to extinction.

GAMMA RAY BURST . . . GAME OVER!

We also face the exotic threat of extinction by gamma rays from space.

When very massive stars reach the ends of their lives and explode, they not only send hot dust and gas across the cosmos in an expanding cloud. They also shoot out deadly twin beams of gamma rays, like lighthouse beams. If the Earth were directly in the path of such a beam, and if the gamma-ray burst happened close enough to us, the beam could rip our atmosphere apart, causing clouds of brown nitrogen to fill the skies.

Such explosions are rare. One would need to happen within a few thousand light-years to do real damage, and the beam would need to hit us very precisely. Thus, astronomers who have studied the problem in detail are not that worried!

SELF-DESTRUCT!

★ We've already done a lot of damage to our planet—without any help from asteroids or gamma rays.

The Earth is home to more than seven billion people.

★ The Earth is suffering from overpopulation.

★ All those extra people mean we will need to grow more food, putting a greater strain on the Earth's natural resources and sending even more gases into the Earth's atmosphere. There's been a lot of argument about climate change. But scientists are clear that the planet is getting warmer and that human activity is the reason for this change. They expect this change to continue, meaning that the world will get hotter and some areas will experience heavy rainfall while others suffer from drought. Sea levels are expected to rise, which could make life very difficult for people who live on coastlines.

★ There are more and more humans on Earth but fewer and fewer other species. Extinction of other animals is a growing problem, and we are seeing whole groups of species disappear from the face of the Earth. It seems a real pity that we are destroying our beautiful and unique planet just as we are learning how it really works.

Globally, nearly a quarter of all mammal species and a third of amphibians are threatened with extinction.

"Exactly! My dad says humans need to look for a new home," said Annie, "just like Freddy does. Pigs need about the same conditions as people, so if we can find a place in the Universe that's suitable for human life, then Freddy would be fine there as well."

"So all Cosmos has to do is find a new home for humanity and we've found somewhere to keep my pig?"

"Precisely!" said Annie happily. "And we can visit him in space from time to time, so he doesn't get lonely and sad again." They both fell silent. They knew that their master plan was rather less than perfect.

"How long is it going take us to find somewhere for Freddy in space?" asked George eventually. "Your dad has been searching and searching for a new place for human beings to start a colony, and he still isn't sure he's found the right place."

"Um, yeah," admitted Annie. "We might—just *might*— want to think about finding Freddy somewhere a bit closer to home, just for now."

"Somewhere on planet Earth would be good," agreed George. "But how are we going to get him to his new home—in space or on Earth? How are we going to carry a great big pig around?"

"Now that is the great geniosity of my brilliant plan!" cried Annie, perking up. "We're going to use Cosmos. If Cosmos can send us on great big journeys across the Universe, then he can take a pig just a short hop across planet Earth. Cosmos, am I right?" she demanded.

"Annie, you are," confirmed Cosmos. "I am so clever and intelligent that I can do any or all of the things you have mentioned."

"But is he *supposed* to?" asked George. "I mean, isn't your dad going to be angry if he finds we've used his supercomputer to transport a pig?"

"Unless you order me to do so," said Cosmos slyly, "I would have no reason to inform Eric that we have taken a porcine adventure together."

"See?" said Annie. "If we ask Cosmos to take Freddy to somewhere he'll be safe, then Cosmos will do it."

"Hmm," said George, still sounding doubtful. He'd been on journeys before where Cosmos had been allowed to pick the destination, and he wasn't sure that the supercomputer always got it right. George didn't want to push his pig through the portal—the amazing doorway into space that Cosmos could open up—and find he'd been sent to a sausage factory. Or the top of the Empire State Building. Or a remote tropical island that would be too hot for Freddy— not to mention too lonely.

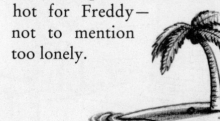

"Cosmos," he said politely, "could you show us the places you'd take Freddy before you actually send him there? Oh, and for the moment, until we find some-where permanent, they all have to be close enough for us to bike to, because I don't think we should keep using you—we might get caught."

"Processing your request," replied Cosmos. When Annie's family had come back from America, Cosmos had suffered a mega breakdown. Eric had managed to fix him, but he had returned with a much more user-friendly attitude. Now, his circuits whirred for a few seconds, and then an image appeared, floating in the air in the center of Eric's study, connected to Cosmos by two thin beams of light.

"It's a map!" said George. "It looks like . . . Hold on! It's Foxbridge!"

"Indeed," said Cosmos. "It is a three-D image. Anything Google can do, I can do better." He harrumphed. "The presumptuous upstarts."

"Oh my, it's beautiful!" sighed Annie. Every feature of the ancient and distinguished university town of Foxbridge was drawn in loving detail on Cosmos's map—each tower, rampart, spire, and quadrangle represented in perfect miniature.

In a corner of one of the courtyards, a little red light was flashing.

"That's my dad's college!" said Annie in surprise. "Where that light is flashing. Why are you showing us Dad's college?"

"My files tell me that pigs need a quiet, dark space with fresh air and some sunlight," said Cosmos. "The place marked is an empty wine cellar at the base of an old tower. It has a ventilation system, so the air is clean, and a small skylight. It hasn't been used for many years, so your pig should be safe and comfortable there for a few days, provided you take the precaution of bringing some straw with him from the farm."

"Are you sure?" said George. "Won't he feel a little cooped up?"

"For a short while your pig will enjoy perfect peace and quiet," replied Cosmos. "It will be a little break for him until you decide where you would like him to be permanently housed."

"We have to get him out of that farm!" exclaimed Annie. "And quickly! He's having a terrible time and we must, must, *must* save him!"

"Can we see the cellar?" asked George.

"Certainly," said Cosmos. "I will open a small window into the cellar so that you can verify the information I have given you."

The map melted into thin air and was replaced by a rectangle of light as Cosmos created his portal: Annie and George had gone through it many times to journey into space. On those occasions, Cosmos had made a door. But if he just wanted to show them something, he drew a small window for them to look through.

"This is so exciting!" exclaimed Annie while they waited. "Why did we never think of using Cosmos to travel around the Earth before?"

The rectangle went dark. George and Annie peered at it more closely.

"Cosmos, we can't see anything!" said George. "I thought you said there would be some daylight. We don't want Freddy to think he's gone to prison!"

Cosmos sounded confused. "I have checked the coordinates, and this is the right location. Perhaps the window has been covered."

"Jeepers!" whispered Annie. "The darkness—it's moving!" Through the window, the blackness seemed to be swaying from side to side.

"Listen!" she hissed. "I can hear voices."

"Not possible," replied Cosmos. "My data tells me that the cellar is no longer in use."

"Then what are all those people doing there?" said Annie in a hollow voice. "Look!"

Staring through the window, George realized she was right. What they were seeing was not a dark room where no light penetrated. It was a throng of tightly packed people, all wearing black clothes. He could just make out shoulders and backs—the crowd seemed to be facing away from them.

"Can they see us?" whispered Annie.

"If they turn around, they will see the portal window," said Cosmos, who had conducted a brief scan of the room. "Although it is entirely inconsistent with logic, probability, and reason, the cellar appears to be filled with human beings."

"Alive ones?" said Annie in a terrified voice. "Or dead ones?"

"Breathing and functional ones," said Cosmos.

"What are they doing?"

"They are—"

"Turning around," interrupted George in horror. "Cosmos, close the portal!"

Cosmos snapped the window shut so fast that no one in the cellar noticed the tiny flash of light. Even if they had, none of them would have guessed that their secret meeting had just been witnessed by two very puzzled kids and an agitated super-computer in an ordinary suburban house somewhere on the edge of Foxbridge.

However, a voice from inside the cellar drifted into the room where Annie and George sat, motionless and shocked. "All hail the False Vacuum!" it said. "Bringer of life, energy, and light." In Cosmos's hurry to shut down the portal before anyone saw it—and them—he had closed the visual monitor but not the audio port, so they could hear but not see the events in the cellar.

A deathly hush followed. Annie and George hardly dared to breathe. Then, as though they were listening to a particularly horrible radio show, the voice continued.

"These are dangerous times!" it hissed. "We may be living through the last days before the Universe itself is ripped to shreds by a bubble of cosmic destruction. Criminal scientists at the Large Hadron Collider will soon begin their new, high-energy experiment. We failed to stop them from using the Collider last time. But now, the situation is far more serious. The moment these crazy fools switch on their machine, a cosmic catastrophe will be unleashed that will exterminate the entire Universe! Their plans to take the work at the Large Hadron Collider to the next level could reduce us all to nothing."

Annie and George heard the densely packed crowd in the room hiss and boo at these words.

"Quiet!" said the voice. "Please—our distinguished scientific expert will explain."

A new voice spoke. This time it was an older, soft-spoken one. "These dangerous lunatics are led by a Foxbridge scientist called Eric Bellis."

Annie squeaked and clapped her hand over her mouth. Eric Bellis was her dad!

"Bellis is masterminding the high-energy collision experiment using the ATLAS detector at the Large Hadron Collider—the LHC. It is about to enter its most dangerous phase. If Bellis achieves the collision energy he intends, then I calculate that there is a significant probability of causing the Universe to spontaneously decay by creating a piece of the True Vacuum.

"If the tiniest bubble of the True Vacuum is created in a particle collision at the LHC, the bubble will expand—

at the speed of light—replacing the False Vacuum and obliterating all matter! All atoms on Earth will dissolve in less than a twentieth of a second. Within eight hours, the Solar System will be gone. Of course, it does not end there . . ."

But the voices from the cellar were fading now as Cosmos struggled to hold the connection.

"The bubble will continue to expand forever," the voice went on in a menacing whisper. "Bellis will have accomplished the unthinkable—the destruction of the entire Universe!" With the last "ssssss" of "Universe" left hanging in the air, the voice was silent once more.

For a moment George, Cosmos, and Annie froze. Cosmos snapped out of it first.

DANGEROUS ENVIRONMENT FOR PIG RELOCATION! flashed up across his screen in big red letters several times.

"We're not sending Freddy there!" agreed Annie, who looked rather dazed. "We're not having our pig spend time with those creepy people! 'Specially not if they're going to be rude about my dad!"

George gulped. What had those black-clad people been talking about? "Cosmos, Annie," he said urgently, "who *were* they?"

Chapter Three

"Who were who?" said a voice as Eric himself pushed open the door to his study, a steaming mug of tea in one hand and a pile of scientific papers jammed under his tweed-jacketed arm. "Hello, Annie and George!" he said. "Enjoying the last day of summer vacation?"

The two friends stared blankly back at him.

"Oh dear! Should I take that as a 'no'?" said Eric. "Is something wrong?" He smiled at them both. Eric couldn't stop smiling these days. If George had to describe Annie's father at the moment, he would have used the words "incredibly happy." Or "incredibly busy." In fact, the busier Eric was, the happier he seemed. Since he had moved back from America, where he had been working on a space mission to try to find traces of life on Mars, the scientist always seemed to be in a rush and always seemed to be enjoying himself. He was happy at home with his family, he loved his new job as professor of mathematics at Foxbridge University, and he was super-excited about the big experiment he was running at the Large Hadron Collider in Switzerland.

The project at the LHC was the continuation of work started by scientists hundreds of years earlier. The aim was to discover what the world was made of, and how the tiny fundamental pieces had fitted together to form the contents of the Universe. To do this, Eric and the other scientists were trying to find a theory that would allow them to understand everything about the Universe. They gave it the simple name the "Theory of Everything": It was the greatest goal in science. If they could only find it, scientists would be able to understand not only the beginning of the Universe but possibly even how—and why—the Universe we live in came about.

Throughout history, people have looked around and tried to understand the amazing things they saw, asking: What are these objects? Why do they move and change like that? Were they always there? What do they tell us about why we're here? Only in the last few centuries have we started to find scientific answers.

Classical Theory

In 1687 Isaac Newton published his *Laws of Motion*, describing how forces change the way objects move, and the *Law of Universal Gravitation*, which says that every two objects in the Universe attract each other with a force—*gravity*—which is why we are stuck to the Earth's surface, why the Earth orbits the Sun, and how planets and stars were created. On the scale of planets, stars, and galaxies, gravity is the architect who controls the grand structure of the Universe. Newton's Laws are still good enough for placing satellites in orbit and sending spacecraft to other planets. But more modern classical theories, namely Einstein's theories of relativity, are needed when objects are very fast, or very massive.

NEWTON'S LAWS

The Laws of Motion

1. Every particle remains at rest, or in motion along a straight line with constant velocity, unless acted on by an external force.
2. The rate of change of momentum of a particle is equal in magnitude to the external force, and in the same direction as the force.
3. If a particle exerts a force on a second particle, then the second particle exerts an equal but opposite force on the first particle.

The Law of Universal Gravitation

Every particle in the Universe attracts every other particle with a force, pointing along the line between the particles, which is directly proportional to the product of their masses and inversely proportional to the square of the distance between them.

Quantum Theory

Classical Theory is fine for big things, like galaxies, cars, or even bacteria. But it can't explain how atoms work—in fact, it says atoms can't exist! In the early twentieth century, physicists realized they needed to develop a completely new theory to account for the properties of very small things like atoms or electrons: quantum theory. The version that sums up our current knowledge of fundamental particles and forces is known as the *Standard Model*. It has quarks and leptons (the component particles of matter), force particles (the gluon, photon, W and Z), and the Higgs (which is needed to explain part of the masses of the other particles, but has not yet been seen). Many scientists think this is too complicated, and would like a simpler model. Also, where is the dark matter astronomers have discovered? And what about gravity? The force particle for gravity is called the *graviton*, but adding it to the Standard Model is difficult because gravity is very different—it changes the shape of space-time.

The Challenge— the Theory of Everything . . .

A theory explaining *all* the forces and *all* the particles— a *Theory of Everything*—might look very different from anything we have seen before, because it would need to explain space-time as well as gravity. But if it exists, it should explain the physical workings of the whole Universe, including the heart of black holes, the Big Bang, and the far future of the cosmos. Finding it would be a spectacular achievement.

With this astonishing prospect in sight, thanks to the new results from the LHC, it wasn't surprising that Eric was in a good mood. Such a good mood, in fact, that he didn't even object to the kids using Cosmos when they weren't supposed to.

"I see you've been on my computer!" He raised an eyebrow, but he didn't look angry. "I hope you didn't get strawberry jam between the keys again," he said mildly, leaning over to look at Cosmos.

"*Where's the best place in the Universe for a pig to live?*" Eric read off the screen. "Ah!" His face cleared. "Now I understand." He ruffled Annie's hair. "Your mom said you were both worried about Freddy."

"We were looking for somewhere else for him to go," said Annie.

"And what did you find?" asked her father, pulling up a rickety old swivel chair so he could sit between Annie and George, who were still gazing wide-eyed at Cosmos's screen.

"Erm . . . well, Cosmos looked around the Solar System but we didn't find anywhere," said George.

"I bet you didn't," murmured Eric. "Can't quite imagine Freddy on Pluto."

"So we thought about taking him to a planet that would be suitable for human life, but we haven't found one yet," continued George.

"Then we looked in Foxbridge instead—to find somewhere close to home to keep Freddy for a few days," Annie burst out. "But we found a group of horrible people in a basement, saying that your experiment at the Large Hadron Collider would exterminate the Universe!"

Suddenly Eric looked furious. "Cosmos!" he barked. "What have you been doing?"

"I was only trying to help," said Cosmos sheepishly.

"Gallumphing galaxies!" Eric didn't look quite so happy now. "What were you thinking of, allowing the kids to eavesdrop on those idiots?"

"They said that you're going to destroy the False Vacuum . . . ," said George slowly. "And that this will make the Universe dissolve. Is this true?"

"No! Of course not! It's a crazy theory," said Eric angrily. "Don't pay them any attention! They're just trying to frighten people because they don't like the work we're doing at the great experiment in Switzerland."

"But they were at your college!" squeaked Annie.

"College schmollege," said Eric dismissively. "They could be anywhere—it doesn't make them any more credible."

"So you *do* know who they are?"

"Not entirely," admitted Eric. "They've concealed

their identities because it's a secret organization—all we know is that they call themselves 'Theory of Everything Resists Addition of Gravity.'"

"Theory of Everything Resists Addition of Gravity . . . ," repeated Annie. "That's T-O-E-R-A-G. That makes TOERAG! Is that really their name?"

Eric laughed. "It's certainly the perfect one for them! They are absolutely a bunch of total toerags."

"What do they want?"

"Last year," said Eric, "TOERAG, as I'm now going to call them, wanted us to abandon the Collider. They said we would create a black hole if we started the experiment. Well, we ignored them and turned it on. Since we're all still here today, you can tell the world wasn't actually swallowed up by a black hole. After that we thought they'd give up. But now they've seized on this 'vacuum' nonsense to prevent us from starting our next experiment, which uses more energy than the ones we've conducted in the past."

"But why?" said George. "Why would they keep on dreaming up crazy theories?"

"Because they don't want us to succeed," Eric explained. "Our goal is to understand the Universe at the deepest level. So we need to know not just *how* the Universe behaves, but *why*. Why is there something rather than nothing? Why do we exist? Why this set of particular laws and not some others? This is the ultimate question of life, the Universe, and everything.

And some people simply don't want us to find that out."

"So this 'bubble of destruction' stuff—it really *is* all nonsense?" George double-checked, just to be sure.

"Complete cosmic cobblers!" exclaimed Eric. "But"—a frown crept over his brow—"despite that, more and more people seem to believe what TOERAG is saying. So we changed the plans for our new experiment, just in case TOERAG decided to surprise us with something nasty."

"So when does it start?" asked George.

"We already started it!" said Eric. "The accelerator is up, the detectors are online, and we even achieved our design luminosity a few weeks ago." The scientist shook his head sadly. "We're keeping it as quiet as we can to stop TOERAG from interfering. Those losers . . . Now, back to the real stuff—where are we going to put Freddy? Cosmos?"

As though trying to make up for his earlier mistake, Cosmos quickly brought up a new image on his screen. It was a beautiful scene, which showed the sun hanging

low over a peaceful wooded valley, with gently swaying trees, wild flowers, and colorful butterflies dancing across the hedges.

"This would be a good place for your pig," suggested Cosmos.

"What about it?" Eric said briskly to George and Annie. "Does that look all right? Would you be happy about Freddy living here?"

"It looks lovely—" George managed to squeeze in. *Where is it?* he wanted to ask, but Eric, who was obviously in a great hurry, had already moved on to the next task.

"Great!" said the scientist, tapping a few commands onto the keyboard. "Now, kids, this is a bit complicated but I think I can make a double portal."

Before the two friends could say anything, Cosmos had opened up a portal to Freddy's farm and Eric had hopped through into the pig pen. The giant pig looked so shocked to see Eric appear out of nowhere that he didn't resist when he was gently pushed through another doorway that Cosmos had created. He trotted away happily into the wooded valley that was still displayed on the screen.

George and Annie watched in amazement as Freddy disappeared through one doorway from the farm, only to reappear in the valley, scampering through the thick grass, his snout twitching excitedly in the fresh country air, eyes sparkling once more.

Eric backed out of the portal doorway and closed it down. "We'll go back in to check up on Freddy very soon," he said. George noticed a faint dusting of straw on his corduroy pants. "I'd better do something about the farm too—stop them from panicking that a pig has escaped and is on the loose."

"What will you say to them?" asked Annie.

"I don't know!" admitted Eric. "But I've managed to explain how a Universe could arise out of nothing, so I expect I can explain away a disappearing pig."

"Pig relocation mission completed. Pig safe and happy in new home. Food, water, and shelter all provided. Threat status to pig—zero," Cosmos flashed up on his screen.

"And now," said Eric in the voice that the children knew meant the subject was firmly closed, "it is time for me to do some work—I need to prepare for the talk I'm giving at the university. And you two should be getting ready for school in the morning."

The two friends slouched reluctantly out of Eric's study. This meant that summer vacation was over. Annie had one evening to do all the preparation homework she had stored up throughout summer vacation. George realized that it was time to go home to his real family. He hoped the babies wouldn't cry constantly the night before he had to go to his new school for the first time.

Annie sighed. "Bye, George."

"Bye, Annie," said George sadly. The next morning they were both starting at different schools: Annie was attending a private school, while George was going to the local school.

"Why do we have to go to middle school?" Annie burst out as they hovered by the back door, neither of them wanting to take the next step. "Why can't we go to a School for Space Exploration? We'd totally be top of the class! No one else has seen the rings of Saturn from close up or nearly fallen into a lake of methane on Titan."

"Or seen a sunrise with two suns in the sky," said

George, thinking of the hot planet in a binary solar system that they'd once visited by mistake.

"It isn't fair!" said Annie. "To make us pretend to be ordinary kids when we're not!"

"Annie!" Eric's voice floated out from his study. "I can hear you! People who don't do their homework don't get to travel into space at all! That's the rule, as well you know."

Annie made a face. "May the Force be with you," she whispered to George.

"And with you," said George, before turning and heading home.

Chapter Four

George's first day at his new school passed in a blur of long corridors and confusing schedules. Again and again he found himself in classrooms for the wrong subjects with older or younger kids.

It was noisy, perplexing, and a bit scary at this enormous school. George wondered if this was how Freddy had felt when he'd moved from the quiet, safe world of George's backyard, first to the small, bustling petting farm and then to the huge, scary new farm. No wonder Freddy hadn't looked happy. On the first day at middle school, even those kids who had been super-confident at George's old school looked lost and worried as they wandered around the huge maze of a building, trying to find the right classrooms. It didn't matter if you hadn't been friends at elementary school—it was such a relief to see a familiar face, rather than all these terrifying grown-up kids—that even sworn enemies suddenly became best friends.

George had only just worked out where he was supposed to be when it was time to go home. He headed out of the gates. Long ago, at his old school, he used to hide in the coatroom every afternoon until everyone else had left, to make sure he wasn't pounced on during his walk home.

But that was before he had learned how to travel across the Universe and unravel great cosmic mysteries. Ever since he'd become friends with Annie and learned about the wonders that surround our planet, George had stopped feeling scared. After all, he'd faced down a mad scientist in a distant solar system; after that, there hadn't been much to be afraid of.

But it wasn't just the journeys that had changed George's life; the knowledge he had gained from those trips had made him feel intrepid. He had used his brain to solve great challenges, and he now knew that he could cope with anything.

As he walked home, George thought about Eric and the adventure with Freddy the evening before. Perhaps, he thought, he could pop over and see Eric to ask if they could check up on his pig. George kicked himself for not asking where Freddy actually was. That valley had looked lovely, but George didn't even know if his pig was still on planet Earth or whether clever Cosmos had transferred him to some other far-off, miraculous place that could support life as we know it. George was sure that Eric knew where Freddy was, but he'd feel happier if he also knew himself.

At home, he dumped his school bag in the hall, then

raced right through his house, only stopping to say a quick hello to his mother and baby sisters and scoop up a pea and cabbage muffin, which he crammed into his mouth in one bite. (George's mom only cooked with the vegetables from their garden; sometimes she had strange ideas about which recipes to use for her home-grown produce . . .) He ran straight out of the back door and into the yard where Freddy had once lived. Jumping through the hole in the fence that led to Annie's backyard, George tore up the path to their back door. He banged on it, but there was no reply. He hammered on it again.

The door opened a few inches. It was Annie, back from school, wearing her new green school uniform.

"Oh, George!" she said. She didn't look entirely pleased to see him.

"Hi, Annie," said George cheerfully. "How's your school? Mine was weird, but I think it might be okay."

"Um, it was all right," she replied, rather quietly. "Did you, er, want something?"

George was surprised. He came over all the time and she'd never before asked him why.

"Er, yeah!" he said, a bit startled. "I was going to ask your dad if he knows where Freddy is. So I can go and visit him."

"Dad's not here," said Annie apologetically. "I'll tell him you asked. I expect he'll e-mail you later."

Then she actually started to close the door in his face. George couldn't believe his eyes. What was going on? Then it all became clear.

"Who is it?" came an older boy's voice from behind Annie.

"Oh, it's, um . . . it's someone who lives next door," said Annie, looking to and fro as though trapped between the two of them. "He wants to see my dad."

She opened the door a tiny little bit wider, and George could now see the other boy. He was taller than both George and Annie, with black spiky hair and skin the color of caramel. Like Annie, he wore a green school uniform.

"Hi!" He nodded to George over Annie's head. "I'm sorry Eric's not here. You'd better go. We'll tell him you came over."

George's jaw dropped in disbelief.

"I'm Vincent, by the way," said the boy casually.

"Vincent also started at my school today," said Annie, not quite meeting George's eye.

"Seriously?" said George in surprise. "You're in sixth grade?"

"No!" Vincent looked annoyed. "Eighth grade. I know Annie from outside school."

"You do?" said George.

"Vincent's dad is a film director," said Annie shyly, but in a way that George just knew meant she was super-impressed by Vincent. "He knows my dad — he made Dad's new TV series."

"A film director," said George, feeling defeated. "Nice. My dad's an organic gardener," he said defiantly to Vincent.

"C'mon, Annie," said Vincent. "We should get rolling."

45

"Mom's taking us to the skate park," Annie told George. "Vincent is a champion skateboarder."

"You roll, then," he said, trying to sound normal. "You just roll along." He turned around and walked back along the backyard path until he reached the hole in the fence. Annie and Vincent were still standing in the doorway, watching him.

George tried to hop casually through the hole in the fence, as he had done so many times in the past. But it didn't quite work and he crashed into the wooden planks instead, falling to the ground with a thump. George couldn't help looking around. Annie and Vincent were still there, which was super-annoying and unfair. When he'd been at the door, they hadn't wanted to open it. Now they wouldn't go away.

With as much dignity as he could manage, he picked himself up and calmly stepped through the gap, trying to behave as if nothing had happened. But inside, he felt wounded and left out. It was only day one of the school

year, and already Annie had a new friend to do cool stuff with.

Where did that leave George?

Now he had no pig, and no Annie either. He suddenly felt empty and alone. He trailed into the house, looking miserable.

A little later that afternoon, when George had done his chores and finished his homework, he decided to go back next door, just in case Eric had come home before Annie and the champion skateboarder Vincent returned.

George found the back door ajar. He pushed it open and sidled in. The house was quiet, dark, and unusually cold, as though, inside, winter had started, while outside it was still only the beginning of autumn. There didn't seem to be anyone home. But if the back door was unlocked, George thought, somebody *must* be home. He listened carefully for signs of life: nothing.

In the gloom, he suddenly noticed a pale blue light coming from under the door of Eric's study. He tapped on it lightly.

"Eric!" he called. "Eric?" He put his ear to the door. There was no sound other than the occasional mechanical beep, which signaled that, inside the study, Cosmos was operational.

George hesitated. Should he open the door? He didn't want to disturb Eric if he was working on an important theory, but it might be his only chance to catch him on his own. Using his fingertips, he carefully pushed open the study door.

Unless you counted Cosmos the supercomputer as a person, there was no one inside Eric's study. Cosmos sat in his usual place on the desk, twinkling away like a Christmas tree, with all his lights on full alert.

From his screen shone the twin beams of light that Cosmos used to draw the space portal—the doorway that had taken George and Annie on so many cosmic journeys. In the middle of the study hung the doorway to space, suspended by the two rays of light and propped open by one of Eric's suede loafers.

Through the crack George could see a desolate

cratered surface under a deep-black sky. He leaned forward to push the door open a little farther so that he could see better, but he was dazzled by brilliant sunlight and had to shield his eyes with his arm.

He stepped back from the portal doorway and looked around Eric's study. Suddenly he spotted his old space suit, left crumpled on an armchair in the corner. Quickly he pulled it on, checked the levels in his air tank, buckled himself in as Eric had shown him, and prepared to step closer to the entrance to space.

With his hands safely encased in space gloves, George pushed at the portal doorway and had a close-up view of the surface of the Moon, the closest celestial body to the Earth. A grayish expanse of dusty ground stretched far into the distance; it was bathed in harsh sunlight that cast strong shadows across the crevasses.

Between the portal and the mountains, George could make out a tiny figure, bouncing enthusiastically toward a crater in the distance. Even though it was wearing an all-in-one white space suit with a fitted space helmet, George could still tell from the uneven, joyous way it was leaping about that it must be Eric. On Earth, Eric tended to shamble along in a distracted haze, but in space he behaved as if he had been set free from earthly cares to enjoy and revel in the wonders of the Universe.

Taking a bold step forward, George crossed the threshold and set first one and then the other boot on the Moon.

As he left planet Earth behind him, he floated up off the ground, the surface of the Moon scrunching under his feet as he landed again. In the Moon's low gravity, he could bounce several feet into the air just by gently pushing off with his space boots.

Q: *When did our Moon form?*

A: It's estimated that the Moon formed over four billion years ago.

Q: *How did it form?*

A: Scientists think that a planet-sized object struck the Earth, causing a dusty hot cloud of rocky fragments to be catapulted into Earth's orbit. As this cloud cooled down, its component bits and pieces stuck together, eventually forming the Moon.

Q: *How big is it?*

A: The Moon is much smaller than the Earth—you could fit around forty-nine Moons into the Earth. It also has less gravity. If you weigh one hundred pounds here on Earth, you would weigh less than seventeen pounds on the Moon!

Q: *Does it have an atmosphere?*

A: No. This explains why the sky is always dark on the Moon, meaning that if you stay in the shade, the stars are visible all the time.

Q: *What explanations did people have for the Moon before scientists discovered how it was formed?*

A: A long time ago, people on Earth believed that the Moon was a mirror, or perhaps a bowl of fire in the night sky. For centuries, humans thought the Moon had magical powers to influence life on Earth. In one way, they were right—the Moon *does* affect the Earth, but not by magic. The Moon's gravity exerts a pull on the oceans, which creates the tides.

51

Q: *Could life exist on the Moon?*

A: The Moon cannot support life—
unless it's wearing a space suit. But
as a consolation prize, evidence is
mounting that the Moon contains
much more water—the prime
ingredient for life as we know it—
than scientists thought just a few
years ago. It's frozen, though, and
any Earth emigrants to the Moon will
need to put substantial effort into
transforming it into its
life-friendly liquid form.

Q: *Has our Moon ever been visited by other
civilizations?*

A: The nearest celestial object to us has been
visited twelve times by astronauts from
Earth. Between 1969 and 1972, twelve
NASA astronauts walked on the surface
of the Moon. Could the Moon have been
visited before human civilization even began on
Earth by extraterrestrials who left deposits behind
them? Could the aliens have come as close as "next
door" to us? It's a (very, very) long shot, but some
scientists on Earth are looking again at Moon rock to
see whether it holds any clues.

"*Hello, Earthlings!*" shouted George, taking a few bounds forward. He knew no one on Earth could hear him, but he just had to say something to mark his first steps on the Moon. Set against the darkness of the sky, his home planet looked like a blue-green jewel, flecked with white clouds. Although both Annie and George had been on exciting cosmic adventures before, this was the first time George had seen his home planet from so close.

From Mars, the Earth had been just a tiny bright fleck in the sky.

From Titan, George and Annie hadn't been able to see the Earth at all through the thick, gaseous clouds on that strange frozen moon of Saturn.

And by the time they'd reached the Cancri 55 solar system, Earth had been hidden from their eyes altogether. Even using a telescope from that distance, they would have only known that the Earth was there from the very slight variable shift in the color of the light coming from our Sun, the star at the center of our Solar System.

On the Moon, however, he was near enough to see the detail of his home planet but far enough away to marvel at its beauty.

After admiring the view, he bounced off in Eric's direction, covering the distance between them very quickly. By the time he reached the scientist, Eric had disappeared into the shallow crater and was looking at a dusty machine, stuck in the bottom of it.

"Eric!" shouted George into his voice transmitter. "Eric! It's me, George!"

"Great gravitational waves!" exclaimed Eric in shock, looking up from the broken-down lunar vehicle. "You gave me quite a scare! I wasn't expecting to meet anyone else up here." He hadn't heard the great shout of joy when George first stood on the Moon as George's voice transmitter had been out of range.

"I came into the study and the door was open," explained George. "What are you doing here?"

"I only meant to go to the Moon for a minute," said Eric rather guiltily. "I wanted to get a little bit of Moon rock to take a closer look at it. I've got this theory about alien civilizations that I want to work on. I figure that if we were visited by aliens sometime in the past—say a hundred million years ago—they would have left traces somewhere. I don't believe anyone has investigated Moon rock to see whether it shows traces of alien visitation. I want to look at Moon rock again with fresh eyes, to see whether there is any signature of life in it. No one has examined Moon rock this way before so I thought I'd get some and try myself. Look what I came across when I was collecting samples! It's a lunar rover!"

"Does it still work?" asked George, quickly scrambling down to where Eric stood. It looked as though a dune buggy had crashed and been abandoned on the Moon. Eric climbed into the driver's seat while George surveyed the rover thoughtfully. "Can you make it go?"

"I expect the batteries are dead by now," said Eric, brushing some dust off the rover with the arm of his space suit.

"There's no steering wheel," noticed George. "How do we drive it?"

"Good question!" Eric wiped his sleeves on his legs, leaving long gray trails of moondust on his white space suit. "There must be some way to switch it on . . ." He fiddled around with a T-shaped joystick between the front seats. But nothing happened. The joystick seemed to be part of a console. Wiping away the lunar dust around it with the thumb of his space glove, Eric uncovered a series of switches with the labels POWER, DRIVE POWER, and DRIVE ENABLE. "Aha!" said Eric happily. "Houston, we have the answer!"

George leaped into the rover alongside Eric. "What happens if you flip those switches?" he asked excitedly. "Can we find out?" He hoped Eric wouldn't turn all grown-up on him and say they shouldn't mess around with someone else's moon buggy. But Eric didn't let him down.

"Yes, we certainly can!" replied Eric. He flipped the switches one at a time and then pushed the joystick, making the rover shoot forward very suddenly. The unexpected movement catapulted them both up into the air and out of the vehicle.

"It works!" Eric cried, climbing back in. "George, could you give the rover a push from behind while

I drive it out of the crater. With the Moon's lack of gravity, it'll be easy."

"Why do *I* have to push?" grumbled George. "Why don't I get to drive it?" But he took up a position behind the moon buggy and braced himself. Eric pushed the joystick forward once more. As he did so, the rover churned its wheels into the ground, showering George with fountains of dust and Moon rock.

"Push harder!" shouted Eric. At that moment George gave an almighty heave, and the lunar rover struggled out of the crater and onto the flat plain above.

"There!" said Eric, brushing his gloved hands together happily and hopping out of the driver's seat. "That's better!" He patted the lunar rover in admiration. "What a piece of machinery! It can't have been used for forty years and it still works! Now that's what I call a car."

"Who does it belong to?" asked George, who was now almost entirely covered in moon rock and dust.

"Left by the Apollo Moon landers, I would think," said Eric. "Look, over there! That must be the descent stage of the Lunar Module." Eric pointed to a four-legged object, squatting in the distance. "This is a piece of space history."

There was a brief silence as they both paused in wonder at what they had found. Then, suddenly, Eric seemed to realize that he was in fact standing on the Moon in the company of his next-door neighbor, a schoolboy called George.

"George, what are you *doing* following me out to the Moon?" he asked.

"I came to ask you about Freddy," explained George. "You didn't tell me where his new home is—I don't even know which planet he's on!"

"Oh, quivering quasars!" exclaimed Eric, hitting himself on the space helmet with his space glove. "Neither do I! We'll have to ask Cosmos. Don't worry—

we know that Freddy is perfectly safe and well—we just need to find out *where*! Was there anything else I forgot?"

Eric was famous for forgetting things, as he freely admitted. He never forgot important matters like his theories about the Universe, but he often forgot day-to-day tasks like putting on his socks or eating his lunch.

"Well, it's not so much that you forgot," explained George. "More that I didn't get to ask you."

"Ask what?" said Eric.

"Your work . . . Looking into the origins of the Universe—is that a dangerous thing to do?"

"No, George," said Eric firmly. "It is *not* dangerous. In fact, I think it would be dangerous if we *didn't* think about the origins of the Universe—if we dealt in speculation rather than in facts about where we come from and what we're doing here. That's dangerous.

"What we're trying to do is understand how this magnificent Universe"—Eric swept his arm around to point at the craggy mountain ranges, the huge dark expanse of black sky, with the distant bauble of planet Earth hanging above the moonscape—"came into being. We want to know how and why these billions of stars, the infinite and beautiful galaxies, planets, black holes, and the incredible diversity of life on planet Earth came about—how did it all begin? We're trying to go back to the Big Bang to find out. That is what the science

of cosmology, studying the origins of the universe, is all about. The Large Hadron Collider will let us re-create the first few moments of time so we can understand better the way the Universe formed.

"What we're doing isn't dangerous and neither is the LHC. The only real danger comes from people who want to stop us: Why don't they want the secrets of the early Universe to be revealed? Why do they want people to be scared and afraid of science and what it could do for us? That, George, is the great mystery to me." Eric sounded mildly frustrated.

"But do you think those people will try to harm you and the other scientists?" asked George.

"No, I don't think so," said Eric. "They'll just sneak around being a nuisance—they're not even brave enough to show their faces, so I don't think we have much to fear from them. Forget them, George. They are just a bunch of losers."

George felt much better now—both about Freddy *and* the origins of the Universe. Suddenly nothing seemed so bad after all. He and Eric turned and bounced back toward the portal, which was still glimmering in the distance. Usually they closed the portal down when they were on a space adventure, but because Eric had only meant to be gone for a couple of minutes, he'd left it propped open with an old shoe.

Before they reached the doorway Eric got his space camera out of his pocket. "We should take our photo! Say, 'Cheese! The Moon is made of!'" he said, holding the camera out and snapping a picture of them as

George made the thumbs-up sign with both hands.

"Will anyone notice that we moved the rover?" asked George as Eric put the camera away.

"Only if they look very carefully," said Eric. "This part of the Moon isn't under constant surveillance. That's why I chose it as a safe place to land."

"Anyway, they should be pleased," George pointed out. "We got their rover out of a hole in the ground and made it work again."

"Hold on a minute," said Eric as he looked up into the sky. "That light over there—*that's* not a comet." A pinprick of light was moving through the dark sky toward them.

"What is it?"

"I don't know . . . But whatever it is, it's man-made—so it's time to go. I've got the rock I need—let's go!"

Together, Eric and George leaped through Cosmos's space portal, back to the place where all their space adventures had begun.

THE CREATION OF THE UNIVERSE

There are many different stories about how the world started off. For example, according to the Boshongo people of central Africa, in the beginning there was only darkness, water, and the great god Bumba. One day Bumba, in pain from a stomachache, vomited up the Sun. The Sun dried up some of the water, leaving land. Still in pain, Bumba vomited up the Moon, the stars, and then some animals—the leopard, the crocodile, the turtle, and, finally, man.

Other peoples have other stories. They were early attempts to answer the Big Questions:

- Why are we here?
- Where did we come from?

The first scientific evidence to answer these questions was discovered about eighty years ago. It was found that other galaxies are moving away from us. The Universe is expanding; galaxies are getting farther apart. This means that galaxies were closer together in the past. Nearly fourteen billion years ago, the Universe would have been in a very hot and dense state called the Big Bang.

The Universe started off in the Big Bang, expanding faster and faster. This is called *inflation* because it is like the way in which prices in the stores can go up and up. Inflation in the early Universe was much more rapid than inflation in prices: We think inflation is high if prices double in a year, but the Universe doubled in size many times in a tiny fraction of a second.

Inflation made the Universe very large and very smooth and flat. But it wasn't completely smooth: There were tiny variations in the Universe from place to place. These variations caused tiny differences in the temperature of the early Universe, which we can see in the cosmic microwave background. The variations mean that some regions will be expanding slightly less fast. The slower regions will eventually stop expanding and collapse again to form galaxies and stars. We owe our existence to these variations. If the early Universe had been completely smooth, there would be no galaxies or stars and so life couldn't have developed.

Stephen

Chapter Five

They tumbled back into the scientist's messy study. In their hurry to avoid being spotted by the mystery satellite, they fell over in a dirty jumble of space suits that were once—but no longer—white.

"The portal is closed," Cosmos informed them. "You have been brought back to your terrestrial home, the beautiful planet Earth."

"Cosmos, you are the most amazing and intelligent computer ever created," said George, who knew how much the supercomputer enjoyed a compliment.

"While I suspect you are flattering me," replied Cosmos, his screen turning rose-pink, as it always did when he blushed, "nevertheless I find your statements to be consistent with reality."

As soon as he had gotten to his feet, George started to wriggle out of his space suit. It now lay on the floor, looking like an empty caterpillar cocoon after the butterfly has broken free. Eric was carefully wrapping up his pieces of precious Moon rock, still wearing his space suit, when they heard footsteps outside the door.

"Quick!" hissed Eric. "Hide your space suit."

George bundled it into the big cupboard in the corner of the study. The air was full of floating fragments of dust, brought back from the Moon.

"Hello!" called Eric in a rather high voice. "Susan, is that you?" After the last adventure, when they had very nearly not made it back from a distant solar system forty-one light-years across the Galaxy, Susan, Annie's mom, had banned the kids from accompanying Eric into space.

"Hello, yes, it's us," said Susan. She didn't come into the study but walked past into the kitchen instead. The sound of thumping feet announced that Annie was back too.

"It was very cool!" she cried, flinging back the study door. "Dad, can I have a skateboard for my birth—?" She stopped in surprise. "Why have you got a space suit on?" she asked. "Why is George here?"

"Shush!" said her dad quickly.

"No! You *haven't* . . . You *have*! Have you been into space without me?" She glared at George.

"You went to the skate park," he said sweetly. "It was . . . very cool. Much cooler than *the Moon*, I should think."

Annie looked like she might erupt. Eric just looked baffled, as though the kids were speaking Vulcan and he had forgotten to plug in his translator.

"I've got to go," said George. "Dinnertime! Bye, Annie. Bye, Eric. Bye, Susan!"

As he dashed out of the back door, Susan called after him, "Don't forget, George! You're coming to the lecture with us tomorrow evening! We've got your ticket . . ."

* * *

The next day, as arranged, George went over to Annie's house before Eric's lecture at the university. Annie was not pleased to see him.

"How was the Moon?" she asked angrily as they strapped on their bike helmets. "Actually, no, don't tell me—I bet that it was totally stupid."

"But you went to the skate park," protested George. "With Vincent. You didn't ask *me* to come!"

"You never said!" Annie muttered, hopping onto her bicycle. "You never said you liked skateboarding! But you *knew* I wanted to go to the Moon. More than anything! It's the place I most want to go to in the whole Universe. And you went without me. You're not my friend."

Even though George knew there was something very unfair about the way Annie was behaving, he was stumped for a reply. Why was she angry with him for doing something with Eric when she was busy anyway, doing something fun with Vincent son-of-the-film-director? But George couldn't ask her that. Instead he just circled mutinously on his bike in

front of their houses until Susan came out, carrying a large cardboard box that she balanced awkwardly on her handlebars.

"C'mon, you two," she said cheerfully, deciding to ignore the fact that Annie and George looked really fed up with each other.

Together, the three of them rode toward the center of town. For several centuries the Math Department had been located in a grand building on a narrow street in the heart of old Foxbridge. But as they turned off the bike path to ride down the street, they found it was so full of people that they had no choice but to get off their bikes and push.

"Who are all these people?" asked Annie as they tried to shove their way through the crowd.

"Let's leave our bikes here," said Susan, pointing to a bike rack. "I don't think we can get any closer to the department with them." They locked up their bikes, then sidled through the crowd of people toward the entrance: A flight of steps led up to a pair of glass double doors with columns on either side. In front of the doors stood a university official, looking anxiously out over the heaving throng below.

"They're all here for your dad's talk!" said George to Annie as he squeezed his way toward the steps after Susan. "Look! They're trying to get into the building!" The crowd surged around them, all pushing forward toward the old stone building

with the inscription AD EUNDEM AUDACTER above the portico.

"What for?" muttered Annie, struggling to keep up with George. "Why would so many people want to come and hear my dad talk about math?"

They ducked and wove their way up the steps to where the official stood guard. Immediately he held out his arm to stop them from going in.

"No entrance to the professor's talk!" he snapped.

"Excuse me," said Susan politely, "but I am Professor Bellis's wife, and this is his daughter, Annie, and her friend George. We've come to help set up the hall for Eric's talk."

"Oh, I am sorry, Mrs. Professor!" said the official apologetically. "We don't usually do security for the Math Department—it's not like this place to cause much of a stir!" He took a handkerchief out and mopped his brow. "But it seems your husband has become pretty famous."

As Susan and the two children turned to look at the waiting people, they heard a sudden commotion from the back of the crowd.

"Stop the criminal scientist!" came the chant. A small line of people dressed in black, wearing masks, were waving banners. "Don't let the advance of science destroy our Universe!"

The official looked horrified and spoke quickly into his two-way radio. "Math Department—send back-up.

Get inside, Mrs. Bellis," he said, opening the door and ushering Susan and the kids through. "We'll deal with the likes of them," he muttered grimly. "We don't tolerate this kind of behavior in Foxbridge. It just isn't done around here."

Chapter Six

Once they were inside, Susan quickly dragged the gaping kids away from the doors and through the entrance hall. They made their way into the big auditorium. "Ignore what's going on outside. Put one of these on every seat," Susan said calmly, giving them each a small cardboard box containing dozens of pairs of dark glasses.

Everything was nearly ready for Eric to take to the stage and give his very first public lecture as the new professor of mathematics at the ancient and very brilliant University of Foxbridge.

Annie and George moved between the rows, carefully putting one pair of glasses on each chair. Annie had for once been really scared by the protestors outside, and she was still trembling slightly.

"Mom, what's going on?" she asked. "Are those the people from TOERAG—that organization Dad was telling us about?"

"I don't exactly know," her mom replied gently. "But they do seem to be objecting to your father's experiments to explore the origins of the Universe. They believe that they are just too dangerous and should be stopped before they can go any further."

"But that's crazy!" said George. "We know that Eric's experiments are safe! And they might show us how the Universe really began. They're, like, the final piece of a jigsaw puzzle that scientists have been working on almost forever! We can't just throw the last piece away before we've seen the whole picture."

By now, they'd worked their way along all the rows from the big double doors at the back of the hall right to the front, where Eric would be speaking. The doors suddenly flew open, and a tall boy zoomed down toward them. He leaped off his skateboard and landed next to George, the wheels still spinning as he caught it in his hands.

"Ta-dah!" he announced.

"Vincent!" squeaked Annie in delight. "I didn't know you were coming. At least I've got *one* friend here!" she added pointedly in George's direction.

"I thought the doors were locked," George muttered grumpily, wishing they still were.

"They just opened them, and"—Vincent pointed

to his skateboard—"I rode straight to the front of the line."

"Have all the people in black gone?" asked Annie. Fans were now streaming into the lecture hall, taking their seats, examining the dark glasses left on the chairs and wondering why they might need them.

"Yup, they've legged it," said Vincent. "Weirdos. What was all that about? 'Criminal scientist'—the morons!" Annie was smiling at Vincent in a way that made George want to pull her hair quite sharply, just to wipe that look off her face.

"One of them tried to talk to me," Vincent added, flipping his board up and down with his left foot.

"What did he say?" asked George.

"I couldn't really make it out," admitted Vincent. "He had a mask on, so I suppose it was like trying to speak through a woolly sock. But it did sound as if he was trying to say a word."

"What word?" asked George curiously.

Vincent eyed him cautiously. "To be honest, buddy," he said, "it sounded like he was saying your name. It sounded like he said 'George.'"

"Why would one of the protesters be saying 'George'?" asked Annie in confusion.

"Maybe he wasn't saying George," said Vincent very reasonably. "Maybe it just sounded like that. Or perhaps that word means something else in I'm-a-crazy-person-who-dresses-up-in-black-for-no-good-reason language. My dad always has trouble at his film premieres," he bragged. "You're really no one at all if you don't have a few loony fans. It's just, like, one of the things that goes with being famous."

"Oh, yeah," said Annie admiringly. "Film premieres. That must be so, like, amazing!"

"Yeah," echoed George vaguely. "Amazing!" He wasn't even being sarcastic. He was too preoccupied with wondering why someone at the protest would be saying his name. There must be a connection, he thought, between the strange people in the abandoned college cellar underneath a tower in Foxbridge and the demonstration outside. Who else would call Eric an evil, criminal scientist other than a faceless group of dark bodies who believed his work had the power to rip the Universe into shreds in a matter of minutes? But how could any of that group know George's name? How could—?

At that moment the lights in the hall flashed on and off a couple of times, and a disembodied voice— which George and Annie recognized as Cosmos—told everyone to take their seats.

"Ladies, gentlemen, kids, and cosmic travelers," the voice went on. "Today we are going on a journey unlike any you will ever experience. Prepare, ladies, gentlemen, and young travelers! Prepare to meet your Universe!"

With that, the whole hall went dark.

Chapter Seven

George, Annie, and Vincent quickly sat down in their seats. They were on the end of the front row, with just one empty chair next to George. The whole of the rest of the hall was packed with people—there wasn't another free spot in the house. In the darkness, they heard the audience shuffle and then fall silent.

"Cosmic travelers," said Cosmos, his voice booming magnificently across the packed hall. "We have many billions of years to cover. You must be ready! Ready to go back to the beginning, ready to understand how it all began.

"Please, put on your dark glasses," he continued. "We will be showing you brilliance and brightness, and we don't want to damage your eyes." Above the heads of the audience, a tiny little pinprick of extremely bright white light had appeared, suspended in the middle of the total darkness. All at once George noticed that the seat next to him was no longer empty. A man had snuck in and sat down. George turned to look at him just as Cosmos projected a huge flash of light that illuminated

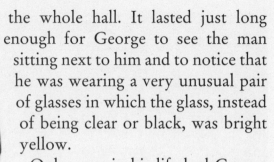

the whole hall. It lasted just long enough for George to see the man sitting next to him and to notice that he was wearing a very unusual pair of glasses in which the glass, instead of being clear or black, was bright yellow.

Only once in his life had George seen such glasses before. When he, Annie, and Cosmos had rescued Eric from the inside of a black hole, the scientist had come out wearing a pair of identical yellow glasses. They hadn't belonged to him, and the mystery of what those odd-looking glasses might have been doing in the middle of a super-massive black hole had never been solved.

"Where did you get those glass—?" George started to ask, but his voice was drowned out by Cosmos.

"Our story begins thirteen point seven billion years ago." As Cosmos spoke, the tiny speck of light hovered above their heads, with the hall in darkness once more. "At that time, everything we can now see in the Universe—and everything we can't see because it is invisible—began as a tiny speck, much smaller than a proton.

"The available space itself was also tiny, so everything had to be crammed together. If we peer back in time as far as we can, conditions were so extreme that physics can no longer describe exactly what was happening at this moment. But it looks as if space as we know it started at zero size thirteen point seven billion years ago, and then expanded."

The dot of light grew very suddenly, like a balloon being inflated. The balloon was slightly transparent, and it was possible to see bright swirling patterns moving all over its surface; otherwise it seemed to have nothing inside.

"This hot soup of stuff," continued Cosmos, "will become our Universe. Note that the Universe is only the surface of the sphere—this is a two-dimensional model of three-dimensional space. As the sphere grows, so the surface expands and the contents spread out.

"Time also began along with space. This is the traditional picture of the Big Bang in which everything, including space and time, comes into being very suddenly at the beginning of history."

Above their heads, the balloon exploded outward, and the audience seemed to be absorbed into its hot, swirling surface. The writhing colors twisted, then dimmed and broke up like a cloud, leaving total darkness in the hall. There were "Oohs" and "Aahs" of wonder.

After a moment, dim, moving patches of light began to appear on the dark ceiling; the patches then took on the shapes of galaxies, spreading out and away from each other until they had all vanished and darkness had returned once again.

"Was it really like this?" questioned Cosmos. "Some scientists wonder whether the Big Bang really *was* the beginning of history. We don't know for sure, but let's pick up the story at a moment just a minuscule fraction of a second after the Big Bang, when the whole observable Universe was scrunched into a tiny amount of space, smaller than a proton."

"Imagine . . . ," said another voice, and a spotlight showed Eric, standing on the stage with a big smile on his face. The audience burst into applause. "Imagine that you are sitting inside the Universe at this very early time . . ."

Imagine that you are sitting inside the Universe at this very early time (obviously, you couldn't sit *outside* it). You would have to be very tough because the temperatures and pressures inside this Big Bang soup are so tremendously high. Back then, all the matter that we see around us today was squeezed into a region much smaller than an atom.

This would be a tiny fraction of a second after the Big Bang, but everything looks much the same in all directions. There is no fireball racing outward; instead, there is a hot sea of material, filling all of space. What is this material? We aren't certain— it may be particles of a type we don't see today; it may even be little loops of "string"; but it will definitely be "exotic" stuff that we couldn't expect to see now, even in our largest particle accelerators.

This tiny ocean of very hot exotic matter is expanding as the space it fills grows bigger—matter in all directions is streaming away from you, and the ocean is becoming less dense. The farther away the matter is, the more space is expanding between you and it, so the faster the matter moves away. The farthest material in the ocean is actually moving away from you faster than the speed of light.

A lot of complicated changes now happen very fast—all in the first second after the Big Bang. The expansion of the tiny Universe allows the hot exotic fluid in the little ocean to cool. This causes sudden changes, like when water changes as it cools to form ice.

When the early Universe is still much smaller than an atom, one of these changes in the fluid causes a stupendous increase in the speed of expansion, called *inflation*. The size of the Universe doubles, then doubles again, and again, and so on until it has doubled in size around ninety times, increasing from subatomic to human scale.

Like pulling a bedspread straight, this enormous stretching flattens out any big bumps in the material so that the Universe we eventually see will be very smooth and almost the same in all directions.

On the other hand, microscopic ripples in the fluid are also stretched and made much bigger, and these will trigger the formation of stars and galaxies later.

Inflation ends abruptly and releases a large amount of energy, which creates a wash of new particles. The exotic matter has disappeared and been replaced by more familiar particles—quarks (the building blocks of protons and neutrons, although it is still too hot for these to form), antiquarks, gluons (which fly between both quarks and antiquarks), photons (the particles light is made of), electrons, and other particles well known to physicists. There may also be particles of dark matter, but although it seems these have to appear, we don't yet understand what they are.

Where did the exotic matter go? Some of it was hurled away from us during inflation, to regions of the Universe we may never see; some of it decayed into less exotic particles as the temperature fell. The material all around is now much less hot and dense than it was, though still much hotter and denser than anywhere today (including inside stars). The Universe is now filled with a hot, luminous fog (or plasma) made mainly from quarks, antiquarks, and gluons.

Expansion continues (at a much slower rate than during inflation), and eventually the temperature falls enough for the quarks and antiquarks to bind together in groups of two or three, forming protons, neutrons and other particles of a type known as hadrons; and also antiprotons, antineutrons, and other antihadrons. Still little can be seen through the luminous foggy plasma as the Universe reaches one second old.

Now, over the next few seconds, there are fireworks as most of the matter and antimatter produced so far annihilate each other, producing floods of new photons. The fog is now mainly protons, neutrons, electrons, dark matter, and (most of all) photons, but the charged protons and electrons stop the photons traveling very far, so visibility in this expanding and cooling fog is still very poor.

When the Universe is a few minutes old, the surviving protons and the neutrons combine to form atomic nuclei, mainly of hydrogen and helium. These are still charged, so the fog remains impossible to see through. At this point the foggy material is not unlike what you would find inside a star today, but of course it fills the whole Universe.

After the frantic action of the first few minutes of life, the Universe then stays much the same for the next few hundred thousand years, continuing to expand and cool down, the hot fog becoming steadily thinner, dimmer, and redder as the wavelengths of light are stretched by the expansion of space. Then, after 380,000 years, when the part of the Universe that we will eventually see from Earth has grown to be millions of light-years across, the fog finally clears—electrons are captured by the hydrogen and helium nuclei to form whole atoms. Because the electric charges of the electrons and nuclei cancel each other out, the complete atoms are not charged, so the photons can now travel uninterrupted—the Universe has become transparent.

After this long wait in the fog, what do you see? Only a fading red glow in all directions, which becomes redder and dimmer as the expansion of space continues to stretch the wavelengths of the photons. Finally the light ceases to be visible at all and there is only darkness everywhere—we have entered the Cosmic Dark Ages.

The photons from that last glow have been traveling through the Universe ever since, steadily becoming even redder—today they can be detected as the cosmic microwave background (CMB) radiation and are still arriving on Earth from every direction in the sky.

The Universe's Dark Ages last for a few hundred million years, during which time there is literally nothing to see. The Universe is still filled with matter, but almost all of it is dark matter, and the rest hydrogen and helium gas, and none of this produces any new light. In the darkness, however, there are quiet changes.

The microscopic ripples, which were magnified by inflation, mean that some regions contain slightly more mass than average. This increases the pull of gravity toward those regions, bringing even more mass in, and the dark matter, hydrogen and helium gas already there are pulled closer together. Slowly, over millions of years, dense patches of dark matter and gas gather as a result of this increased gravity, growing gradually by pulling in more matter, and more rapidly by colliding and merging with other patches. As the gas falls into these patches, the atoms speed up and become hotter. Every now and then, the gas becomes hot enough to stop collapsing, unless it can cool down by emitting photons, or is compressed by collision with another cloud of matter.

If the gas cloud collapses far enough, it breaks into spherical blobs so dense that the heat inside can no longer get out—finally, a point is reached when hydrogen nuclei in the cores of the blobs are so hot and squashed together that they start to merge (fuse) into nuclei of helium and release nuclear energy. You are sitting inside one of these collapsing patches of dark matter and gas (because this is where the Earth's galaxy will be one day), and you may be surprised when the darkness around you is broken by the first of these nearby blobs bursting into bright light—these are the first stars to be born, and the Dark Ages are over.

The first stars burn their hydrogen quickly, and in their final stages fuse together whatever nuclei they can find to create heavier atoms than helium: carbon, nitrogen, oxygen, and the other heavier types of atom that are all around us (and *in* us) today. These atoms are scattered like ashes back into the nearby gas clouds in great explosions and get swept up in the creation of the next generation of stars. The process continues—new stars form from the accumulating gas and ash, die, and create more ash. As younger stars are created, the familiar spiral shape of our Galaxy—the Milky Way—takes form. The same thing is happening in similar patches of dark matter and gas peppered across the visible Universe.

Nine billion years have passed since the Big Bang, and now a young star surrounded by planets, built from hydrogen and helium gas and the ash from dead stars, takes shape and ignites.

In another four and a half billion years the third planet out from this star will be the only place in the known Universe where human beings can comfortably exist. They—you—will see stars, clouds of gas and dust, galaxies, and cosmic microwave background radiation everywhere in the sky—but not the dark matter, which is most of what lies there. Neither will you be able to see anything of those parts that are so distant that even the CMB photons from there have yet to arrive, and indeed there may be parts of the Universe from which light will never reach our planet at all.

This is our beautiful Earth . . .

Chapter Eight

As Eric finished his talk and the lights went up, the whole audience jumped to their feet, bursting into loud applause, which rang and rang around the lecture hall.

Modestly Eric took a few bows and then stumbled off the stage, where he was immediately mobbed by eager fans, flash bulbs popping, and television cameras shadowing his every move. The crush around him was so dense that Annie and George had no hope of getting anywhere near him. The pressure of the crowd drove them slowly backward, away from where Eric was standing.

Annie's cheeks were pink with excitement. "Amazing!" she kept saying to no one in particular. "That was amazing!" she babbled on to Vincent, who seemed dazed, as though he had looked into the heart of a burning star and now couldn't return to reality on planet Earth.

George suddenly heard a polite but pointed cough near him, and turned to see the man who had taken the seat beside him standing there. George realized that

he was very old, with white hair and a soft drooping mustache. He wore a suit of pressed tweed with a vest, and a watch chain looped across the front of it. The old man gripped George's arm.

"You were sitting next to Eric's daughter," he whispered urgently. "Do you know Eric?"

"Yes . . ." George tried to back away. The old man's whiskers were almost tickling his face.

"What is your name?" asked the old man.

"George," said George, still trying to move backward.

"You must get him," replied the mustachioed man

urgently. "I must speak to him. It is very important."

The old man was now wearing an ordinary pair of clear glasses, making George wonder if he had imagined the yellow ones earlier.

"But who are you?" he asked.

The old man frowned. "You mean you don't know?"

George thought very hard. Had he met this man before? Somehow he didn't think so. But there was something familiar about him—something about the way he spoke—that was trying to ring bells in George's mind.

"You recognize me, don't you?" persisted the old man. "Go on, tell me my name."

George racked his brains but he just couldn't think who this might be. Embarrassed, he shook his head.

"Really?" The man's face fell. He was obviously disappointed. "I was very well known in my day," he said sadly. "Every school child knew of my theories. You mean, you have never heard of Zuzubin?"

George grimaced. He felt awful. "No, I'm sorry, Professor Zuzubin . . ." He couldn't finish.

"I am sad," said the old professor sorrowfully, "to hear this. I was Eric's tutor, you know!"

"Yes!" cried George in relief that he had something positive to say. "That's where I've seen you before—in the photo of Eric at the university! You're his great teacher!"

Professor Zuzubin didn't look any happier. "Eric's

great teacher . . . ," he murmured. "Yah, that is how I would be remembered. That is what they would think of me if . . ." He seemed to check himself. "Never mind," he said decisively. "Bring me Eric. I will be waiting in his office. Now hurry, George!"

George had to fight his way through to Eric, who was busy answering questions from the fans grouped around him in starstruck clusters. "Stop pushing!" they hissed to George as he tried to barge through. He saw that Eric had unplugged Cosmos, folded him up, and tucked him under his arm.

Finally George got close enough to whisper into his ear. "Eric," he said, "Professor Zuzubin is here and he wants to speak to you. He's says it's very important."

"Zuzubin is here?" said Eric, turning to George in surprise. "Here? In this lecture hall? Are you sure? *The* Zuzubin?"

"Zuzubin," George confirmed as people wanting to talk to Eric shoved and pushed him. "He's waiting for you in your office. He says it's urgent."

"Then I must go!" said Eric. He clapped his hands together loudly. The hall fell silent. "Thank you all for listening!" he told his fans. "Please come back next month, when we will be discussing baby black holes and the end of the Universe. Good evening, ladies, gentlemen, and children!"

Eric left the lecture hall to another huge burst of applause, with George following behind him, a frown on his face. There was something about Professor Zuzubin—whether it was the yellow glasses or the strange way he had said Eric's name—that made George feel uneasy about him. Whatever was about to happen to Eric, George needed to know . . .

"What," said Professor Zuzubin, slamming a photograph down on Eric's desk, which made all the half-drunk cups of tea, unopened envelopes, scientific papers, and piles of books perched on it jiggle nervously, "is the meaning of this?"

"Professor Zuzubin," said Eric, turning red and fidgeting. "I . . . I . . ."

George gazed at him in amazement. He had never seen Annie's father being told off before.

Professor Zuzubin just stood there, watching his former pupil. "Eric Bellis, I know this has something to do with you. Kindly explain yourself."

George sneaked a look at the photo. It showed a grayish cratered surface. But in the middle of the fuzzy photo seemed to stand two indistinct figures in space suits.

"Oh dear," murmured Eric.

"Oh dear indeed," said Professor Zuzubin.

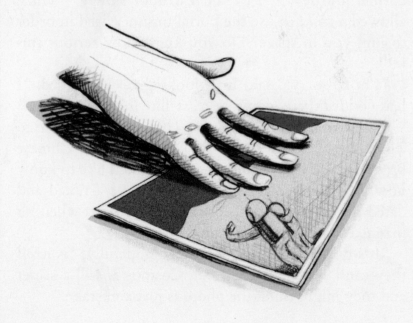

"This is all *my* fault," said Eric immediately. "You can't blame George."

"*George!*" Professor Zuzubin exploded. "Now you're taking children out into space? What is next? Taking a trip to the Moon with a whole school party? What were you thinking?"

"No, it was just me," said George bravely. "I followed Eric out to the Moon because I wanted to ask him a question. He didn't invite me to go there; I went out all by myself." As soon as the words were out of his mouth, George realized that his explanation actually made everything sound much worse.

"So you left the space portal unsecured during a cosmic journey . . . ," said Zuzubin slowly, "which allowed a *child* to use the portal unsupervised in order to join you in space? Do you know how serious this is?"

"I'm so sorry," said Eric, looking very ashamed. "I had no idea there would be a satellite in that location."

"You were very careless. This photo," retorted Zuzubin, "was sent to me by Dr. Ling at the Chinese branch of the Order of Science. He would like to know how a Chinese satellite managed to take a timed and dated photo of two astronauts on the Moon when no manned spacecraft have visited it since 1972."

"It's not that bad," said George hopefully, "is it? If they can't see the portal, then Cosmos is still a secret and they might think the photo is just a mistake."

"A *mistake*?" yelled Zuzubin. "You used the super-computer to take a little day trip to the Moon and got caught, and you think this counts as a *mistake*?"

"Don't shout at George," said Eric, rallying a little. He took a swig from one of his cold cups of tea, which seemed to fortify him. "I admit—we went to the Moon using Cosmos so I could investigate a theory I'm working on. I needed some Moon rock as a sample. But that's it! End of story."

"No!" said Zuzubin, turning red. "Not end of story! For now this photograph is still highly confidential—Dr. Ling has managed to see to that—but if it gets out, then we are all in very deep trouble. You knew that Cosmos could only be an effective tool for scientific discovery if we kept his existence a complete secret. You knew what might happen if he became public knowledge. You are the guardian of the world's greatest supercomputer. And yet you . . . you . . ."

He looked so angry, George thought his head might explode like an erupting volcano.

"This has come at the worst possible time for the Order of Science to Benefit Humanity," he continued, more calmly now.

The Order of Science to Benefit Humanity was a special and very distinguished group of scientists who had come together to make sure that science was used for good and not evil. Eric was a member—and so, in fact, were George and Annie. George had become the youngest member ever to join during his adventures with Eric and the black hole.

"You must have seen the protest today outside your lecture," Zuzubin ranted on. "You must realize that T.O.E. Resists Addition of Gravity is gathering strength right now."

George noticed that he made a great effort to call the protest group something other than TOERAG, which George thought was rather odd. After all, the name seemed to suit them extremely well, so why didn't the mysterious cosmologist want to use it?

"They are getting braver," Zuzubin went on. "They have never appeared in public before today. But they know people worldwide are turning away from science, and so they are gaining in confidence. In this atmosphere, if the public finds out through your foolish actions that we kept a supercomputer secret, they will start to ask what else we keep from them—perhaps the Collider really *is* dangerous, they will say. Perhaps none of us should be allowed to continue our work? Our lives in science could be over. Science itself could be over."

George thought Eric was about to burst into tears. He had never seen him so upset.

"What can I do?" said the scientist, wringing his hands. "How can I make this better?"

"We have called an emergency all-members meeting," said Zuzubin, checking the round silver watch looped across his vest, "of the Order of Science to Benefit Humanity. You must leave immediately and take Cosmos with you. They will review all the activities that Cosmos has undertaken while he has been in your care to see whether your use of the supercomputer has been justified."

George and Eric both gulped. The thought of the Order of Science looking through Cosmos's log and finding that he had recently been used to transport a pig was not a comfortable one.

"You will explain to the Order what you have done," said Zuzubin.

"That could be very awkward . . . ," murmured Eric, still thinking about Freddy.

"And they will decide whether you will remain as Cosmos's guardian and custodian. I have arranged your transport."

Eric turned pale. "You mean, they want to take Cosmos away from me?"

"They can't do that!" cried George. "That's wrong!"

"We shall see," said Zuzubin. "Eric, you must leave now. You will be collected from your house."

"Where am I going?" asked Eric.

"To the great experiment."

"I'm coming with you," said George. "I'm a member of the Order of Science. I should be there."

"Certainly not," thundered Zuzubin. "You will stay here. This is not a matter for children."

"Zuzubin is right," said Eric gently. "This doesn't concern you, George."

"But where are you going?" he asked. "Where is the meeting? When will you come home?"

Eric gulped. "The Large Hadron Collider," he said quietly. "I'm going back to the beginning of time."

With that, the three of them filed silently out of Eric's office and headed for the double doors at the entrance. Eric and George went out onto the street, but as George looked back through the glass, he saw that Zuzubin was not following them. Instead, the old professor disappeared down the stairs by the front door. That's curious, he thought. Where was Zuzubin going?

"Eric," said George as the scientist unlocked his bike, "what's underneath the Math Department?"

"*Underneath?*" said Eric. He looked completely dazed. "I haven't been down there since I was a student."

"What's down there?" persisted George.

"A load of old junk, I should think. Old computers, mostly. I don't know . . ." Eric shook his head. "I'm sorry, George. I've got a lot on my mind right now. Find your bike and we'll ride home."

Chapter Nine

Back at Eric's house, Annie was whooping with glee at how well his lecture had gone.

"Vincent said you were awesome," she said happily. "He said you totally rocked!"

But the happy atmosphere didn't last long. One look at Eric and George told Susan that something very unexpected must have happened. She took Eric into the study and closed the door. It didn't make any difference—through the thin walls the two children could still hear every word Annie's parents said.

"What do you mean?" they heard Susan ask Eric once he'd broken the news. "How can you be leaving for Switzerland tonight? It's the beginning of term. What about your students? What about *us*? You promised you would help with our anniversary party! It's been planned for ages—don't let me down, Eric. Not again."

"What's going on?" whispered Annie to George. They were hovering in the kitchen.

"A satellite took a photo of us on the Moon," George told her. "It was sent to some ancient professor by the

Chinese branch of the Order of Science. And now your dad is in trouble. He's got to go to a meeting at the Large Hadron Collider right away: He has to explain what happened to see whether they will let him keep Cosmos."

Annie turned green. "We might *lose* Cosmos?" she hissed.

"Susan," said Eric in the next room, "I'm really sorry."

"You *promised* me," said Susan. "You promised me you wouldn't mess our lives up anymore!"

Annie and George didn't want to listen but they couldn't help hearing. Every word was horribly clear.

"If I don't go now, I will *definitely* lose Cosmos," said Eric.

"Cosmos!" retorted Susan angrily. "I'm so sick of that computer! It's been nothing but trouble."

"That's not true," protested Eric feebly.

Annie ran out of the kitchen and burst into the study. "Stop!" she announced dramatically. "I can't stand it! Don't argue anymore!! Stop it! Just stop it!"

George stood frozen in the kitchen. For the first time since he'd known the family next door, he would have given anything to be back in his own house with his own parents. Even though his baby sisters made lots of

noise and his mom cooked weird food, he just wanted to get out of Annie, Susan, and Eric's lives and back into his own.

"Annie, please," said Susan. "This is between your father and me."

"*Are* they going to take Cosmos away?" Annie asked her dad, who seemed to have drifted off into a universe of his own.

"What?" said Eric, sounding startled.

"You weren't even listening, were you?" sighed Susan. Suddenly she sounded totally defeated. "I was talking to you and you were thinking about science."

"I . . . I . . ." Eric couldn't deny it.

"Maybe it would be better if you *did* lose Cosmos," said Susan rashly. "I hope they take that dratted computer away from you, then we can get back to being a normal family."

"Mom!" Annie cried out in horror. "You don't mean that."

"Oh yes I do," said Susan. "If the Order of Science doesn't destroy that blasted machine, I'll do it myself."

After that, it got very awkward and frosty in the house. Eric stomped upstairs to pack, followed by Annie, full of suggestions of what to say to the Order of Science. "Annie! I will handle this by myself!" George heard her father say in an unusually loud voice. "Stay out of it! This is none of your business!"

As George stood there, still stuck in the same spot in the kitchen, he heard Annie run down the stairs and into Eric's study, slamming the door behind her. The sound of noisy sobs rang through the house.

"Annie . . ." Susan tapped gently on the study door.

"Go away!" shouted Annie. "I hate you! I hate you all!"

Susan came into the kitchen, her face pale and drawn. "I'm so sorry, George," she said in a tired voice.

"That's okay," said George. But it wasn't. He'd never heard grown-ups arguing like that and it made him feel sick.

"You should go home now," said Susan kindly.

Eric appeared in the doorway. "Here, take this . . . ," he said, handing George the hamster, Pooky, in its cage.

"Oh—and this. It's a souvenir," he added sadly. "In case they come and confiscate all my space stuff while I'm away. I thought you'd want to keep it." It looked like a large off-white duvet had been stuffed into a knapsack. But George knew exactly what it was: Eric was giving him his space suit.

"Are you sure?" he said, shouldering the knapsack and taking the cage in both hands. The hamster, Pooky, was no ordinary pet. He was in fact the only nano supercomputer in existence. Designed by Dr. Reeper, Eric's former colleague, Pooky was almost as powerful as the great Cosmos himself.

At least, in *theory* Pooky was that powerful—the only problem was, Eric had no idea how to operate him. The nano computer was disguised as a very lifelike small furry animal, but it had no control panel and didn't respond to any commands or instructions. Without his creator, Dr. Reeper, supercomputer Pooky was entirely useless. Eric had hoped to link him up with Cosmos, but this plan had failed. Instead, Pooky had been living quietly in a spacious hamster cage where he cleaned his whiskers, slept, and ran on his wheel—not much to challenge the world's second most intelligent computer . . . But until Dr. Reeper returned from his extended vacation at a distant physics institute, there was nothing Eric could do with Pooky. Except keep him safe—and secret.

Apart from Reeper, only George, Eric, and Annie knew about Pooky. Which, George suddenly realized, meant the Order of Science to Benefit Humanity could have no idea that a second supercomputer existed. They only knew about Cosmos.

"Bye, George," said Eric. "Good luck."

"What about Annie?" asked George. The sobbing had now stopped.

"I'll ask her to text you," said Susan. "When we have things figured out."

George slipped out of Annie's kitchen door and back across the yard, hopping through the hole in the fence.

In the darkness, his house glowed with a welcoming, familiar light. The solar-powered electricity generator his eco-friendly dad had rigged up didn't provide a strong current, and the battery it fed was often rather flat in the evenings.

George opened the back door and went into the kitchen, where his mother, Daisy, was processing vegetable purée for the babies. The smell of home overwhelmed him. His mother turned and smiled.

"Have you come home? To stay, I mean?" she asked, seeing her eldest child hovering in the doorway, clutching a large hamster cage and a knapsack. A lump came into George's throat. He nodded.

"I'm so glad," Daisy said gently. "I know it's been difficult for you here with the girls . . ." The twins were snoozing in two rush baskets on either side of the stove, their long, dark eyelashes sweeping down over petal-perfect cheeks. "It will get better," she went on, hugging George, "when they're a little older. And not quite so noisy."

One of the twins—George still wasn't quite sure which—laughed in her sleep, a pretty tinkling sound, like stardust falling to Earth.

"You'll be amazed when they're older—you won't be able to imagine what life was like without them."

George's dad, Terence, was standing in the doorway, watching. George realized that his parents had never said anything about the huge amount of time he spent at the house next door, and suddenly he loved them even more for not mentioning it.

"It's good that you're back, George," his dad said gruffly. "We missed you. Here, let me help." He took the hamster cage and peered in at the world's second most powerful computer who, like the babies, was now asleep. "Who's this . . . ?"

"That's Pooky," said George. "Can he stay in my room?"

His parents smiled. "Of course," Daisy said. "What a dear little thing! A little smaller than that funny old pig."

"I'll take him upstairs," said Terence.

With that, George climbed the stairs to his own room and went to sleep in his own bed, the curtains left open a crack just in case he should wake up in the night and look out to see a shooting star.

Chapter Ten

In the quiet, dark street below, a long shiny black car pulled up in front of Eric's house. The driver got out and rang the doorbell. A white-faced Eric was waiting behind the front door, clutching a very small suitcase, with Cosmos in a laptop bag. He turned on the threshold to say good-bye. Susan and Annie hugged him tightly.

"I have to go," he said. His eyes burned like two dying stars in his pale face.

"Good luck," said Susan quietly. "Eric, please be careful! Please! Watch out for yourself. There are bad people out there, and they don't like you."

"Hush, hush, I'll be fine!" said Eric, trying to sound cheerful. Now that he was actually leaving, Susan and Annie couldn't be angry with him anymore. "In a few days I'll be back and we'll all be laughing about this! It's just a silly misunderstanding—once I've had a chance to explain, everyone will be fine. I'll be home before you know I've gone! Maybe even in time for the party!"

"Bye, Dad!" said Annie, her bottom lip wobbling.

"C'mon, Professor." The driver was getting impatient. "Get in the car, sir. We're on a schedule."

Eric turned away and climbed into the sleek vehicle, the driver carefully shutting the door on him. The windows were made of dark glass, so Annie and Susan didn't see the tear running down his cheek as he sat, alone with his computer, on the soft leather seat.

The car rolled away down the street, the powerful engine purring. They drove in silence to a nearby airfield—it was a private strip where only a few planes landed and took off each day. A few words from the driver to the guard at the gate, and the car was through, heading right onto the airfield.

A jet was waiting in the brilliant light of a full Moon, the small staircase folded down so that Eric could get right out of the car and into the plane. He climbed aboard, and found that he was the only passenger.

After only a few minutes the pilot's voice came over the loudspeaker. "Good evening, Professor Bellis. It is our great honor to be flying you this evening. We will

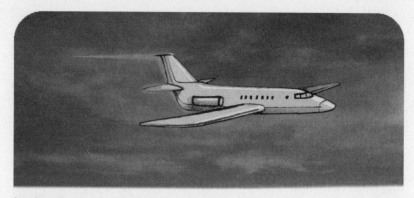

be landing at an airfield near the Large Hadron Collider in about an hour and a half. Could we ask you to fasten your seat belt for the journey?"

With that, the little plane accelerated down the runway and smoothly lifted its nose until they were flying through the night sky toward what could be the end of Eric's career.

Even though George had fallen into a deep sleep the moment his head touched the pillow, it didn't last long. After what felt like just a few seconds, he found himself sitting bolt upright in bed, cold sweat trickling down his back. His sleep had been full of confused dreams in which people in black were chasing Freddy through thick orange grass on a faraway planet where the sun was green. "Stop the criminal pig!" they shouted in his nightmare. George tried to call out, to tell them to leave Freddy alone, but he could only manage a terrified croak.

Waking in his bedroom, George was struck by a horrible thought. If Eric came back without Cosmos, he would never find out where Freddy had gone! Eric hadn't told him where the pig's new home was because he had still needed to look it up on Cosmos. If Cosmos was lost to them, then so was Freddy! What if the computer had sent him right out to the farthest reaches of the Universe? That would mean he'd be moving farther and farther away from him . . . George might never see him again, and it would be his own fault for not taking better care of his pig in the first place.

THE EXPANSION OF THE UNIVERSE

The
astronomer Edwin
Hubble used the one-hundred-inch
telescope on Mount Wilson, California, to
study the night sky. He found that some of the
nebulae—fuzzy, luminous specks in the night sky—are
in fact galaxies, like our Milky Way (although the galaxies
could be of widely varying sizes), each containing billions
and billions of stars. And he discovered a remarkable
fact: Other galaxies appear to be moving away from us, and
the farther they are from us, the faster their apparent speed.
Suddenly, humanity's Universe became much, much larger.

The Universe is expanding: Distances between galaxies are
increasing with time. The Universe can be thought of as
the surface of a balloon on which one has painted blobs
to represent galaxies. If one blows up the balloon,
the blobs or galaxies move away from each
other; the farther apart they are, the
faster the distance between
them increases.

THE REDSHIFT

Very hot objects in space,
like stars, produce visible light,
but as the Universe is constantly expanding,
these distant stars and their home galaxies are
moving away from Earth. This stretches their light as
it travels through space toward us—the farther it travels,
the more stretched it becomes. The stretching makes visible
light look redder—which is known as the cosmological redshift.

George lay there in bed, feeling miserable and sorry for himself—and for Freddy. It occurred to him that a midnight muffin and a glass of milk might provide some consolation. So he slipped out of bed and tiptoed very lightly downstairs in his pajamas, knowing his parents would not be happy if he woke up the babies when they were sleeping.

But halfway down the stairs he heard a noise; it came from the dark, and supposedly empty, ground floor. George froze, too scared to go any farther down but not wanting to go back upstairs either in case he drew attention to himself. He listened really carefully, straining his ears for any faint sound.

Just as he was starting to think that he must have imagined the noise, he heard it again. It was quiet but distinct—footsteps, as stealthy and careful as his own. Outside, the Moon was full and shining so brightly that it seemed almost like day in the silvery light that flooded in through the downstairs windows. From where he stood, pinned by fear against the staircase wall, George saw a long shadow pass the foot of the stairs and continue into the kitchen. He heard the back door open and

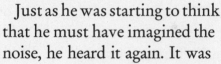

close as the catlike footsteps padded away.

As noiselessly as he
could, George snuck
back up the stairs to
look out of the window
into the garden. By the
light of his old friend the
Moon, George saw the
long shadow creep down to the end of the yard, where
it seemed to float over the back fence and disappear.
George's blood was pumping so hard in his ears that he
felt dizzy. He ran into his parents' bedroom and shook
his dad awake.

"*Rumppfff!*" his dad snorted, turning over.

"*Dad!*" hissed George urgently. "Dad! Wake up!"

"Grugfmp!" Terence was talking in his sleep. "Ban
the bomb! Save the whale! Meat is murder!"

George shook him again.

"Ban the whale! Murder the bomb! Save the meat!"
Terence carried on sleep-talking while, beside him,
Daisy was snoring softly, her head underneath the
pillow.

Finally he woke up. "George! . . . Is it the babies?"
Terence groaned. "Do they need feeding—again?"

"Dad, I saw someone!" George told him. "There was
someone in the house! I saw them climb over the fence
at the end of the yard."

Terence grunted unhappily but got heavily to his feet. "Good luck finding anything to steal in this place," he muttered to himself. "Good luck finding anything at all." But he went downstairs to check, coming back with a serious but very sleepy face.

"The back door was open," he said to George. "I've locked it now. It was probably just a cat, you know. Go back to sleep now, before the babies—"

At that moment they both heard a wail from one of the cribs. "Oh no," groaned Terence. "There goes one . . ." Another baby wail joined in. "And there goes the other. Back to bed, Georgie. See you in the morning."

The next day at school, George's head was pounding. He slumped over his desk, hardly able to keep his eyes open. His dad had decided not to report anything to the police—nothing had been stolen, and anyway, Terence was sure that it was some kind of animal, probably a cat, that had nosed its way into the kitchen in search of food.

George didn't agree: The footsteps he had heard were too heavy to belong to a cat, unless it was the size of a leopard. It was much more likely that it had been a person. But he didn't argue with his dad. He gave a huge yawn. It was exhausting, trying to work all this out.

"Are we keeping you up?" said George's new history teacher pleasantly.

"No, sir," said George.

"Then kindly get out your textbook and turn to page thirty-four."

George fumbled in his bag and found the book. He opened it at the page he had marked to read for homework the evening before but, in all the excitement of Eric's talk, completely forgotten about.

Someone else, however, had got there before him. Tucked into that very page was a note, folded in half and with his name written on it in a familiar old-fash-ioned, curly script. Heart sinking, George unfolded the piece of paper, and read:

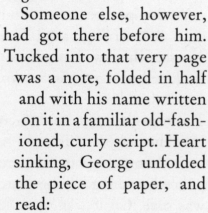

George,
Evil is at work in the Universe. Our friend Eric is in danger. We must speak. Do not try to contact me by any means. I will come to you.
Courteously yours,
Dr. R.

George felt a chill creep down his spine. His bag had been downstairs the night before. He'd left it on the table in the living room. That meant the shadow he had seen and the footsteps he had heard must have belonged to none other than Dr. Reeper, Eric's old enemy.

Why visit me? thought George in horror. *Why not visit Eric?*

As soon as he'd asked himself the question, he knew the answer. Eric wasn't there—by last night he'd already gone, taking Cosmos with him. And Pooky, the nano supercomputer that strange Dr. Reeper might have expected to find at Eric's, had been upstairs in George's house, where Reeper hadn't dared venture. If he had intended to visit Eric, he would have already been too late to find him. So he came looking for George instead. If Reeper was creeping around in the dead of night, then he must have something very important to tell him. George knew he needed to find Reeper and ask him what was going on. But could he trust him?

Annie, George knew, would say "No way!" Reeper had got them into deep cosmic trouble twice before. But he had turned out okay in the end: He'd saved all their lives when they had got stuck on a distant moon with no way back. And once they'd returned to planet Earth, Reeper had sworn to put his dark past behind him. He wanted to be friends with Eric, he'd said. He wanted to work as a real scientist again, and not live in the shadows any longer.

Judging by the note that George had found in his textbook, it looked as though Reeper had information that would help Eric. George had a thousand questions running through his head, the first of which was: How on earth would he ever find Reeper?

"If I was a crazy ex-scientist, where would I be?" he thought to himself. At least, he *meant* to think it to himself, but it soon became apparent that he'd said it out loud.

"I don't know where a crazy ex-scientist might be," replied his teacher mildly. "But if I was George Greenby, I would be on page thirty-four right now, and about to give my teacher the answer to the question written on the board."

The rest of the class tittered. "Sorry, sir," said George,

NASA/courtesy of nasaimages.org.

Our beautiful Earth, with our one Moon.

Above:
A setting last quarter crescent
Moon and the thin line of the
Earth's atmosphere; photo taken
from the International Space Station.

Right: Exploring the surface
of the Moon in a lunar rover.

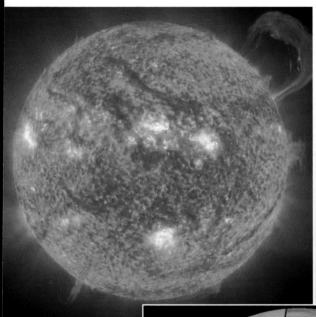

Our Sun.

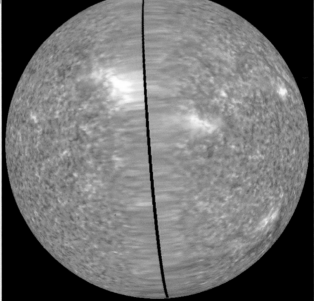

Twin probes beam back views of our Sun— both front and back! This amazing composite image was created in February 2011.

LOOKING AT OUR EARTH FROM SPACE

The Semien mountains of Ethiopia, Africa.

NASA/courtesy of nasaimages.org.

The Great Sand Dunes National Park and Preserve in Colorado.

The horrifying results
of the tsunami and
earthquake in
March 2011 in Japan.

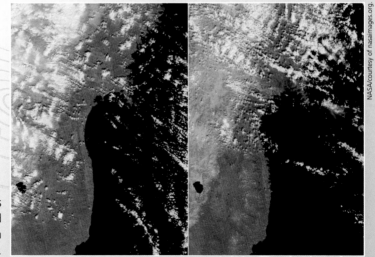

NASA/courtesy of nasaimages.org.

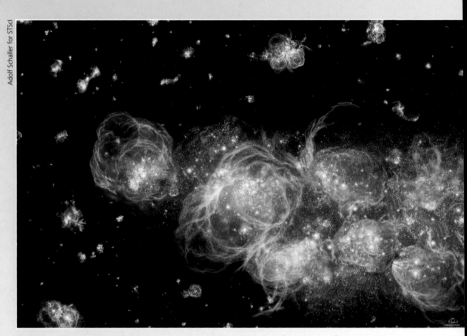

Adolf Schaller for STScI

Hubble's deepest views of the cosmos suggest that the first stars after the Big Bang lit up the heavens like a fireworks display.

NASA, ESA, R. O'Connell (University of Virginia), F. Paresce (National Institute for Astrophysics, Bologna, Italy), E. Young (Universities Space Research Association/Ames Research Center), the WFC3 Science Oversight Committee, and the Hubble Heritage Team (STScI/AURA)

A young glittering collectic of stars—NGC3603 in the constellation Carina, twent thousand light-years away.

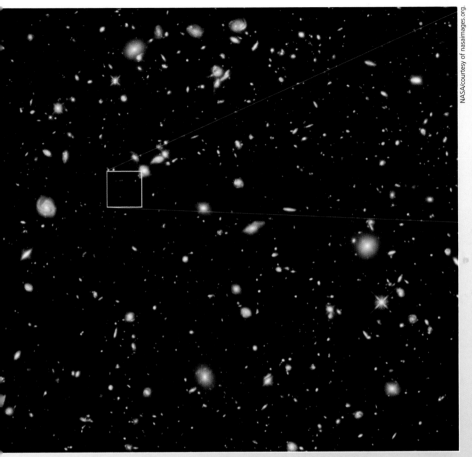

The image at the top of the page is marked: NASA/courtesy of nasaimages.org.

e faint red blob—an infrared image—shows one of the very earliest galaxies ever seen in our Universe.

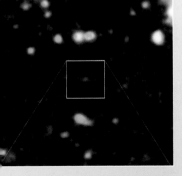

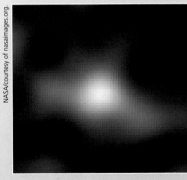

NASA/courtesy of nasaimages.org.

A tiny building block of today's giant galaxies, this compact galaxy existed only 480 million years after the Big Bang.

In the massive galaxy cluster Abell 1689
astronomers use the latest technology t
chart this map of dark matter—matter
that cannot be seen directly.

and for the next thirty minutes he tried to make his brain return to 1066 and all that, instead of focusing on the evil at work in the Universe.

But he found it almost impossible. One thought kept flashing through his mind, as clearly as if Cosmos had shouted it in huge red capital letters:

ERIC IS IN DANGER.

Chapter Eleven

After school, George rode around Foxbridge on his bicycle before going home. It was very unlikely that he would just run into Reeper on the street, but he didn't know what else to do. And then he remembered Cosmos's map of Foxbridge. The basement! If he could find the basement where the secret meeting had been held, he might be able to discover more information about TOERAG. He just *knew* that Reeper's message had something to do with those people in black.

Had Reeper been at the demonstration?

Was Reeper the figure in black who had tried to talk to Vincent?

George pedaled very fast. He knew Foxbridge really well, and Cosmos's map had shown him exactly where the secret basement was.

When George got there, he realized that this was, of course, Eric's college—the one where he and Reeper had been students of the great Zuzubin. Reeper, Zuzubin, and Eric were all members of the same college community.

Zuzubin, thought George. *Zuzubin*. Why did he seem to be everywhere and nowhere all at the same time?

The huge gates of Eric's college were closed and bolted, but a little door cut into the wood of the main entrance was left open for students to come in and out. George hopped through, only to find a fierce-looking porter, the guardian of the college, waiting for him.

"I have something for Professor Bellis," George lied, not knowing what else to say.

"Leave it at the desk," growled the porter, who had just finished straightening every single blade of grass in the bright green lawn behind him. He'd dusted down the marigold petals in the herbaceous borders, swept all

the paving stones, and polished the brass door knockers, so the last thing he wanted was a scruffy schoolboy messing up his perfect courtyard. "College is closed."

The porter stood there, glaring at George over his handlebar mustache, giving George no choice but to back out and go home. After he'd had a snack George went next door to see Annie, but he found only Susan, Annie's mom, who appeared frazzled for a change. Normally it was George's mom who looked like she'd got out of the wrong side of bed. This time, Susan had the messy hair, mismatched clothes, and worried eyes.

"Annie's not here," she told George. "She's gone to a karate lesson with Vincent. Apparently he's a black belt."

Of course he is, thought George. He would be.

"I would ask you in," continued Susan, looking stressed, "but I've been trying to get everything ready for this big party we're having on Sunday and Annie and I need to go to my sister's tonight so I'm very busy. And look! This window is broken—we don't know how. There's glass every-where."

George's heart sank. "Did that happen last

night?" he asked. He didn't want to tell Susan that his house had received a midnight visit too. She looked anxious enough as it was.

"It looks like it," she replied. George thought she was going to cry. "We didn't hear anything — and nothing's been taken. It's very strange."

"Is Eric back soon?" he asked to try to cheer her up.

"I've hardly heard from him. But he says the big meeting is tomorrow night," said Susan. "And he hopes they'll figure everything out so that he can fly back the morning after. I must leave now, George. I can't stay any longer."

With that, she shut the back door, and George heard the sound of the key turning in the lock, followed by the sharp noise of bolts being shot across. He sighed. There was nothing more for him to do here so he went home.

As he came into the kitchen, his father had just switched on the radio for the news.

"*Could the Universe be swallowed by a bubble of destruction, leaked from the Large Hadron Collider?*" said the newsreader in a cheerful voice. "*That's the big question on everyone's lips this evening.*"

"George!" said Terence. "Do you know anything about this?"

"Shush!" said George. "Please, Dad, I need to listen!"

The news report continued:

"*A dramatic statement released today by anti-science*

group The Theory of Everything Resists Addition of Gravity claims that the new experiment at the Large Hadron Collider could be extremely dangerous! In an open letter to the Universe, Theory of Everything scientists state that the experiment is reckless and unsafe, as it may produce a tiny amount of something called the True Vacuum.

"According to Theory of Everything sources, our existence in the Universe depends on the False Vacuum, which could be destroyed as a result of the high-energy experiments scheduled to begin shortly at the Collider. Within eight hours, Theory of Everything estimates, the bubble of destruction could have ripped our whole Solar System apart! Professor Eric Bellis, leader of the Collider Experimental Group, was this evening unavailable for comment. However, in the last few minutes a statement has been issued on behalf of the those working with him: 'The Collider is perfectly safe and no one should be afraid of the advances of science.'

"And now, in other news—"

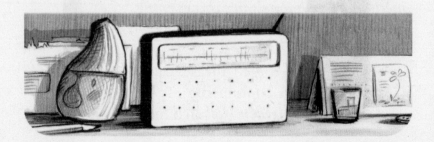

VACUA

What is a vacuum, and what does it have to do with vacuum cleaners?

A vacuum means a space so empty it doesn't even have air in it. So if we pumped all the air out of a room, for example, we would create a vacuum.

A vacuum cleaner uses an air pump to create a puny sort of "would-be" vacuum that helps it to sweep up all the particles of dust when you're cleaning your house. But you couldn't use a vacuum cleaner to make the sort of vacuum that we're talking about here. You'd need something with a much more powerful pump for our experiment.

> VACUA IS THE PLURAL OF VACUUM

> The vacuum in the beam pipes of the Large Hadron Collider is as empty of gas molecules as some regions of outer space!

127

Removing all the air particles from a room is not an easy job. Even a room completely empty of *atoms* still contains *radiation*:

- Infra-red photons emitted by the warm walls of the room

- radio photons from TV transmitters

- microwave photons left over from the Big Bang

- other particles whizzing through from space (e.g. neutrinos produced by the Sun)

- It also would still contain dark matter!

What if we could remove the radiation by cooling down the warm walls? Then the room would be emptier than the space between galaxies! But it would still contain something called *quantum fields*. These are what are behind photons, neutrinos, electrons, and the other particles. Physicists call the lowest energy state of the quantum fields the *vacuum state*, and it is this state—the state without any observable particles—that would now fill our imaginary room.

If we could look closely enough, we would also be able to see tiny ripples in space-time and gravity called *gravitational waves*.

So, although we may think that the room has been completely emptied when we pumped the air molecules out, close up, this vacuum actually buzzes with activity!

Put energy into a vacuum state (physicists would say *excite* it), and particles (and antiparticles) appear. It is thought that the vacuum is the state of *lowest energy*. There may be many other vacuum states with equally low energy—when excited they would create familiar-looking particles. In the early Universe, when the temperature was much higher, space may have existed for a little while in a *false vacuum* state with higher energy, whose particles would seem exotic today. As the temperature fell, this false vacuum would have decayed into our current lower-energy vacuum. A *true vacuum* is one which really does have the lowest possible energy.

There is no reason to think that any experiment on Earth could kick us into a different vacuum!

Terence switched off the radio. "Is this true?" he said somberly to George. "Are we really at risk from Eric's experiments?"

"No!" exclaimed George. "Of course not! Eric wants to help human beings, not destroy them!"

"Then why are they saying those things about him on the radio?"

"I don't know," said George. "Someone wants to stop him from making discoveries, so they've invented this bogus theory about the True Vacuum. I have to find out why! I need to help Eric."

"You need to do your homework," said his dad seriously. "And stay away from Eric and his family for now. I don't want you getting mixed up in this—do you understand me, George? If there is a reasonable explanation, we'll wait to hear it from Eric himself. Until then, you keep out of the way. Do you promise me?"

"I promise," said George. But even though he hated to deceive his father, he had his fingers crossed behind his back.

The next morning was Saturday, and George was lying sprawled on top of his bed, fully dressed and wondering what to do next, when his phone rang. Now that he had started at middle school, his parents had finally let him have a cell phone.

"Annie!" He had never been more pleased to hear from her. He'd sent hundreds of texts the evening before, and called her, but she hadn't replied.

"Did you hear what they said about my dad on the news?" she asked him.

"Erm . . . yes," said George cautiously. It must be horrible, he thought, to have a famous dad. "Has he called you?"

"Nope," sniffed Annie. "He hasn't texted or e-mailed or anything. Just nothing. But all the over the Internet, people are saying he's a dangerous lunatic and must be stopped from doing any more experiments because he's about to destroy the whole Universe. All I know is that Mom says he's got this big meeting with the Order of Science tonight at seven thirty and she hopes he's coming home after that."

"I had a weird note," confessed George. "From Reeper."

"From *Doctor Reeper*?" screeched Annie. "What does it say?"

"It says that your dad is in danger and that evil is at work in the Universe."

"What use is that?" she exclaimed. "We *know* that already! Why can't he say something helpful for a change? Did you speak to him?"

"Nuh-uh," said George. "He didn't, like, give a number to call. Just a note, Reeper-style, written on parchment in loopy old writing. Like he'd dipped a feather pen in blood or something."

"How very Reeper-the-Creeper," said Annie in a hollow voice.

"I tried to get Pooky working," George continued.

"And did you?"

"Nuh-uh," said George again, looking over at Pooky's cage. The hamster supercomputer was snuffling around in some hay, his little eyes blue and blank and empty of any meaning whatsoever. For once he wasn't running crazily in his hamster wheel, spinning round and round and round for hours on end. "I even got in touch with Emmett last night, and tried connecting remotely, but he said he couldn't figure it out either." Emmett was Annie and George's computer genius friend in America.

"Rats!" said Annie sadly. "Or rather—hamsters! If the master geek can't do it, then we've got no chance."

"Emmett did say one thing about Pooky, though," George told her. "He said that he thinks all this running in the wheel is Pooky's way of keeping his CPU cool while he's computing something. Something about coolant pumping around his brain when he's active."

"So Pooky is active, but we can't get him to work!" Annie sighed. "That's so frustrating! Why won't Pooky help us?"

George didn't get to answer, because at that moment a piercing high-pitched noise burst out of the hamster's cage.

"Was that the babies?" asked Annie, who'd heard it on the other end of the phone.

"Not the babies . . . ," said George slowly. "I think that noise came from Pooky."

Pooky was standing on his hind legs with his nose pointing directly up at the ceiling. His paws scrabbled wildly in the air and he screeched again, a bloodcurdling sound that seemed too loud to come from such a small animal. Suddenly Pooky's head swung around and he turned to glare at George with his little hamster eyes, which had turned from sky blue to flashing yellow.

"What's going on?" said Annie sharply.

"Pooky's having some kind of fit!"

But then Pooky opened his mouth. "George," he said, in a voice that sounded like a rusty nail scraping across a blackboard. "George."

"*Who said that?*" Annie screamed into the phone.

"Pooky . . . ," whispered George, whose hair was prickling on the back of his neck. "Pooky just spoke!" Pooky, as far as he knew, had never before uttered a single word. Unlike Cosmos, he was a silent super-computer. Until a few moments ago.

But the voice Pooky used hadn't been the voice of a hamster, or even a computer: It was the voice of a human being, and one whom they both knew quite well.

"Reeper!" said Annie. "Pooky spoke to you in the voice of Doctor Reeper!"

"George," said Pooky again, this time more clearly, "you must help me."

"What do I do?" said George to Annie, panicking.

"Find out what he wants," she urged. "But don't be fooled! Remember what he did to us before!"

"How can I help you?" asked George, horribly aware that he was now having a conversation with an electronic hamster.

"You must come and meet me," said Pooky, his eyes flashing. "You must travel into space to find me. We need to talk."

"Reeper, is that you?"

"Who else could it be?" said the hamster in Dr. Reeper's voice.

"The last time we met," said George bravely, "you wanted to abandon us to run out of oxygen on a moon forty-one light-years away from Earth. And the time before, you tried to throw Eric into a black hole."

"I've changed," said Pooky simply. "I want to help you."

"Why should I believe you?"

"You don't have to, but if you don't come and find out what I have to say, Eric will never come home . . ."

The thought of Freddy, abandoned and alone in a strange place forever, flashed through George's mind as well.

"Why can't you tell me now?" he said, seizing the little hamster with both hands. "What's happening to Eric?"

"Eric is in grave danger . . . Only you can save him, George. Only you. Meet me. Pooky will bring you to me. I don't have much time. You must leave immediately. Good-bye, George. See you in space!"

"Reeper!" George shouted at the hamster. "Reeper! Come back!" But Pooky's eyes had turned blue again, and George realized that the connection had been lost.

"What did he say?" Annie yelled into the phone.

At that moment the hamster gave a shudder, and a tiny pellet dropped out of his furry backside.

"He said"—the phone was shaking in George's hand—"that I must come and meet him in space!"

"But where?" cried Annie. "Where in space are you supposed to meet him?"

"He didn't say. He didn't tell me where to come or how to get there."

"Try Pooky again!" ordered Annie.

George picked up the little hamster and gently pressed all over his tiny furry body to see whether there was some hidden switch they hadn't yet found. But the hamster just gazed back at him with the same empty expression as before.

"I'm on my way over," said Annie.

"No, don't come!" said George. "There isn't time." He picked up the tiny pellet that Pooky had deposited on the floor of his cage. It was a screwed-up ball of paper. George unraveled the pellet, which turned out to be a long thin ribbon of paper with a line of numbers on it, ending in a capital H. "There seems to be another message . . . Perhaps it's the destination . . . ," he said slowly, remembering a letter that Dr. Reeper had once sent to Eric, giving him the coordinates of a distant planet he wanted Eric to visit. The string of numbers reminded him of the way Reeper had written the location of that planet—the snag being that it had turned out not to exist, and Reeper had actually sent Eric right into the path of a super-massive black hole. "Maybe this is where I'm supposed to meet Reeper . . ."

"But how will you get there?" asked Annie. "And how do we know it will be safe? Maybe you're going to fall into a black hole!"

"I can't talk now," said George, who had the phone jammed between his shoulder and his ear as he jumped off the bed and wrenched open his cupboard to find the space suit that Eric had given him as a souvenir of their cosmic journeys.

Pooky was stirring again, his blue eyes slowly

changing color—the signal, George now knew, that he was about to spring into action.

"I'm coming over," said Annie firmly. "I'll be there really fast—I've got my bike with me. Don't go anywhere before I get there."

"Sorry, Annie," said George. "I don't have time to wait." Pooky had sat bolt upright and his eyes were now flashing red; they shot out two little beams of light that stopped halfway across the room and started spinning, forming a brilliant circle that whizzed round and round like Pooky's hamster wheel.

"George!" said Annie into the phone. "Don't hang up!" At that moment he was struggling into his space suit. "Don't go into space alone!"

"I don't have a choice!" George shouted before he put on his space helmet so he could still speak with his normal voice rather than through the voice transmitter. "If I don't go now, we won't know what Reeper has to tell us! Annie, I have to go . . ."

He put the cell phone down on his bed. In front of him, Pooky's circle of light had grown. Beyond it he saw a silver tunnel, which led off into the distance with no sign of what lay on the other side. George put on his space helmet and took a deep breath from his air tank. Through the transmitter, he could hear Reeper's voice again.

"George," he rasped. "George—enter the tunnel of light."

"Where are you?" asked George, trying to sound brave. He didn't feel brave. He had never been so scared in all his life. His blood felt like it had frozen in his veins, but his heart was pounding so loudly that he thought his ears might explode.

"I am at the other end, waiting for you," said Reeper. "Follow the tunnel, George. Come to me."

When George had stepped through Cosmos's portal on his previous journeys around the Universe, he had usually been able to see where he was going on the other side. But this time there was only the shimmering silver tunnel, which curved away without showing where it was taking him.

What would he find at the other end? A parallel Universe? Another place in time? Did the tunnel bend away because it followed the curvature of space-time, leading to some mysterious destination far away from the Earth's gravitational field? What lay in wait for him at the other end? There was only one way to find out.

"If you want to save Eric," whispered Reeper, "you must go on this journey. Just take the step, George. The tunnel will bring you to me."

"*George!*" Annie screamed from the phone on the bed. George could still pick up noises around him, thanks to the external microphone in his helmet. "I can hear Reeper as well! Don't go!"

George hesitated. Then he heard another voice speaking on the phone. It was Vincent.

"George, buddy," he said. "Don't go by yourself! It isn't safe. Annie's told me about the portal and Doctor Reeper. You mustn't do this."

What? thought George, feeling miffed. What was Vincent doing with Annie at her aunt's house? All the time he'd been talking to Annie, Vincent had been listening in? Vincent knew about the portal and Cosmos and Dr. Reeper? Vincent knew all the secrets that he and Annie had faithfully sworn never to tell anyone? And now Vincent, karate champion and ace skateboarder as well as Annie's new BFF, was telling *him* what to do?

So Vincent thought he couldn't handle it, did he? Vincent thought he wasn't brave enough to save Eric, George's mentor and teacher and Annie's dad? "I'll show you, Vincent," he muttered to himself. "And I'll save you, Eric, even if no one else will.

"Good-bye, Earth people," he

went on haughtily. "I am going into space. I may be gone for a while."

He stepped forward toward Pooky's wheel of light, which quickly sucked him into the tunnel as though he had dived down a waterslide at the park. George whooshed headfirst through the silver tunnel, his arms stretched out in front of him, turning this way and that as he was whisked out of his bedroom to an unknown location.

George didn't have time to think—he was traveling at immense speed through a blur of shining light on his way to meet his former deadly enemy, Dr. Reeper, somewhere out there in the great cosmic expanse that makes up our Universe.

From a place already light-years behind him, he thought he heard Annie scream, the sound echoing around his space helmet: "*Noooooo!*"

But it was too late. George was gone.

Four-Dimensional Space-Time

When we want to go somewhere on Earth, usually we only think in two dimensions—how far north or south, and how far east or west. That is how maps work. We use two-dimensional directions all the time. For example, to drive anywhere you only need to go forward (or reverse), or turn left (or right). This is because the surface of the Earth is a two-dimensional space.

The pilot of an airplane, on the other hand, isn't stuck to the Earth's surface! The airplane can also go up and down—so as well as its position over the Earth's surface, it can also change its altitude. When the pilot is flying the plane, "north," "east," or "up" will depend on the airplane's position. "Up," for example, means away from the center of the Earth, so over Australia this would be very different from over Great Britain!

The same is true for the commander of a spaceship far away from the Earth. The commander can choose three reference directions any way he or she wishes—but there must always be three, because the space in which we, the Earth, our Sun, the stars, and all the galaxies exist is three-dimensional.

SPACE, TIME, AND RELATIVITY

Of course, if we have something we need to get to, like a party or a sports event, it isn't enough to know *where* it will be held! We also need to know *when*. Any event in the history of the Universe therefore needs four distances, or coordinates: three of space and one of time. So to describe the Universe and what happens within it completely, we are dealing with a four-dimensional space-time.

Relativity

Einstein's Special Theory of Relativity says that the laws of nature, and in particular the speed of light, will be the same, no matter how fast one is moving. It's easy to see that two people who are moving relative to each other will not agree on the distance between two events: For example, two events that take place at the same spot in a jet aircraft will appear to an observer on the ground to be separated by the distance the jet has traveled between the events. So if these two people try to measure the speed of a pulse of light traveling from the tail of the aircraft to its nose, they will not agree on the distance the light has traveled from its emission to its reception at the nose. But because speed is distance traveled divided by the travel time, they will also not agree on the time interval between emission and reception—if they agree on the speed of light, as Einstein's theory says they do!

This shows that time cannot be absolute, as Newton thought: That is, one cannot assign a time to each event to which everyone will agree. Instead, each person will have their own measure of time, and the times measured by two people that are moving relative to each other will not agree.

This has been tested by flying a very accurate atomic clock around the world. When it returned, it had measured slightly less time than a similar clock that had remained at the same place on the Earth. This means you could extend your life by constantly flying around the world! However, this effect is very small (about 0.000002 second per circuit) and would be more than canceled by eating all those airline meals!

Chapter Twelve

George shot out of the other end of the tunnel, skidding facedown along a stretch of bare rock. His vision was still blurry from the bright, swirling lights of the silvery tunnel. For a second he saw stars before his eyes; then he lifted his head and saw thousands more of them, burning brightly in the black sky around him.

As he peered up, he saw something else. A large black boot appeared in front him, and then another. George rolled over and looked up at a figure in a black space suit looming over him, its face hidden by the darkened glass of the space helmet. It didn't make any difference. George didn't need to see his features to know that this was Dr. Reeper: the thwarted scientist and madman was on the loose in the Universe once more.

Behind Reeper's head there was an immense expanse of sky, so dark that his shape seemed to blend into it. Beside him, George could see nothing but bare gray rock pitted with great craters. He struggled to sit up, his muscles jellified by the journey.

"You can stand," said Reeper drily. "I picked an

asteroid with enough mass that you wouldn't float off."

When George had landed on a comet, on his first space journey with Annie, they'd had to tether themselves to the potato-shaped ball of rock and ice because its gravitational force was not strong enough to keep them on the surface. While the comet had been mostly dust, ice, and frozen gas, this asteroid was bigger, and made from much denser material: The gravity here seemed to be holding George firmly in place.

"Where are we?" he wondered, staggering a little as he got to his feet.

"Don't see anything you recognize?" asked Reeper. "No lovely blue-green planet hanging in the distance, just waiting for you to save it?"

George could see nothing but stars. The mouth of the tunnel had disappeared entirely, leaving him no escape from Reeper and this strange, rocky place.

"Of course you don't," continued Reeper. "You wouldn't recognize much of your own Galaxy if I'd taken you out into the Milky Way. But you are no longer in your home Galaxy. You've journeyed farther than ever before."

"Are we in another Universe?" asked George. "Was that a wormhole?"

"No," said Reeper. "That's my updated version of the portal. A doorway seems terribly old school, don't you think? Eric always was such a traditionalist. You wouldn't think it, would you? His theories tore up everything we thought we knew about the Universe, and yet when it comes to designing a portal, he models it on his own front door.

"This, George, is Andromeda."

The Andromeda Galaxy (also known as M31) is the *nearest large galaxy* to our own Milky Way, and together they are the largest objects in our Local Group of galaxies. The Local Group is a group of at least forty nearby galaxies that are strongly influenced by each other's gravity.

 At 2.5 million light-years away, Andromeda is not actually the closest galaxy to us (that title probably goes to the *Canis Major* dwarf galaxy), but is the closest with a comparable size and mass.

 Current estimates suggest that the Milky Way has more *mass* (including dark matter), but Andromeda has more *stars*.

 Andromeda has a *spiral* shape, like the Milky Way.

 Like the Milky Way, Andromeda has a *super-massive black hole at its center*.

 Also like the Milky Way, Andromeda has several (at least fourteen) satellite dwarf galaxies in orbit around it.

Unlike most galaxies, light received from Andromeda is blue-shifted. This is because the expansion of the Universe— which makes galaxies move away from each other—is being overcome by gravity between the two galaxies, and Androm- eda is falling toward the Milky Way at around 300 kilometers per second (186 miles per second). The two galaxies may collide in around 4.5 billion years, and eventually merge— or they may just miss. Colli- sions between galaxies are thought not to be unusual— the small Canis Major dwarf galaxy appears to be merging with the Milky Way right now!

"Another galaxy . . . ?" said George in awe.

"Our neighbor," confirmed Reeper, sweeping an arm around him. "This is, if you like, the galaxy equivalent of the house next door. Given the size of the Universe, it might as well be. Notice anything?"

"The stars look the same . . . ," said George slowly. "This asteroid looks like an asteroid. I suppose we must be orbiting a star, so we're in another solar system. It's not so very different from being in the Milky Way."

"Yes, indeed," agreed Reeper. "Remarkable, isn't it? Close up, no two pieces of rock are exactly the same. No two planets, no two stars, no two galaxies. Some regions of space contain just clouds of gas and dark matter, but in other places you find stars, asteroids, and planets. So much variety! Yet here we are, two and half million light-years away from Earth, and things don't look that different. This asteroid could be in our own Solar System; those stars could be in our own Milky Way. The variations here are the same as in our own Galaxy. What do you think that means, George? Answer me that and I'll tell you why we are here."

"It means," said George, thinking about Eric's lecture, "that everything everywhere was formed in the same way, from the same material and by the same rules, but the tiny fluctuations at the beginning of time caused everything to turn out a little bit different from everything else."

UNIFORMITY IN SPACE

In order to apply General Relativity to the Universe as a whole, we usually make some assumptions:

> every location in space should behave in the same way (*homogeneity*)

> and every direction in space should look the same (*isotropy*).

This leads to a picture of the Universe that is

> uniform in space

> starts with a Big Bang

> and then expands equally everywhere.

This picture is strongly supported by astronomical observations—what we can see in space through telescopes on the ground and in space.

Yet the Universe can't be *exactly* uniform in space, because this would mean that structures like galaxies, stars, solar systems, planets, and people couldn't exist. A pattern of tiny *ripples* over the uniformity is needed to explain how the first patches of gas and dark matter could begin to collapse, so that the laws of physics could go on to create stars and planets.

Because the gas and dark matter start out nearly uniform, and because we believe the same laws of physics apply everywhere, we expect that all galaxies form in a similar way. So distant galaxies should have similar types of stars, planets, asteroids, and comets to those that we can see in our own Milky Way.

Where the initial tiny ripples came from is not yet completely understood. The best theory at the moment is that they came from microscopic quantum jitters that were magnified by a very rapid early expansion phase—called *inflation*—that took place during a very tiny fraction of the first second after the Big Bang.

"Well done! I am glad to know that one of my ex-pupils at least can show that he has benefited from his education."

"Why have you brought me here?" asked George bravely. "What is it this time?"

"I don't think I like your tone." Reeper now sounded more like he had when he'd been a teacher at George's old school.

"I don't think I like being catapulted into space by a talking hamster," George shot back at him.

"Of course," said Reeper hastily. "I can see that was a bit of a surprise. But I had no other way of contacting you."

"Oh, really?" said George. "Didn't you break into my house at night and leave a note in my schoolbook?"

"Yes, yes, I did," said Reeper. He seemed unusually nervous, unlike the Reeper of old, who was always totally confident of his evil powers. "I was trying to attract your attention. I couldn't find Eric next door so I came and left a note for you instead."

"Why didn't you just come and talk to me, if it was so important?"

"Because I can't," said Reeper in frustration. "I can't go anywhere or do anything—I'm trapped. Since I slipped away to your houses the other night, they've put me under even closer surveillance. They don't know I visited you, but they know I went somewhere and it has made them suspicious. That's why I had to meet you in space. It's the only safe place for us to talk. I couldn't possibly have contacted you—and certainly not Eric—by earthly means. I would have blown our only chance of stopping them."

"Who is it who's watching you?" asked George.

"Them," said Reeper. "TOERAG. They are everywhere." He looked around as he spoke, as though they might be floating past the asteroid in this unknown part of the Andromeda galaxy. "They are the unseen, the dark force. They are all around us."

"I think that's dark matter you're thinking of," said George. "The invisible material that makes up twenty-three percent of the known Universe."

"George," said Reeper earnestly, "you are so right. They are humanity's dark matter. You can't see them, but you know they are there by the effect they have on the Universe around them."

For once, he seemed to be speaking from the heart—if indeed he actually had one.

"Were they the people in black at Eric's lecture?" demanded George.

"That was a few of them. There are many more—they are a vast network. I was there too at the demonstration—I couldn't get near you so I tried to alert you via that boy but it didn't work."

"I knew it!" said George. "I knew it was you! But I couldn't work out why. I don't understand why TOERAG is doing this. Why would it be so bad if

Eric discovered the Theory of Everything? Why would it be so dangerous to understand the origins of the Universe?"

"For you and me it would be a great step forward. For TOERAG it would be a terrible, wounding blow."

"Because of the True Vacuum," asked George, "and what it might do?"

"The leaders don't really believe that the Universe will be ripped apart in a growing bubble of destruction, leaked from the Large Hadron Collider," Reeper told him. "That's just a terrible apocalyptic prospect they use to frighten people into joining their organization so that their network keeps on growing. What they're really scared of is something very different."

"Such as?"

The asteroid sped onward on its orbit, circling a very bright young star that was a few billion years younger than our Sun. As George watched, two hundred-yard-

long chunks of rock smashed into each other with the energy of a nuclear explosion. A cloud of pulverized dust expanded outward. This young solar system was a very violent place, with many such chunks hurtling around the central star. Eventually planets would form and vacuum up all the debris left lying around after these collisions, but for now, it was a chaotic, dangerous place to be. Although, thought George, from what Reeper had to say, it sounded like almost anywhere in the Universe was a better bet than planet Earth right now.

"The leaders of TOERAG are convinced that Eric's experiments will eventually have other results," said Reeper. "Once we have the Theory of Everything, they believe that scientists will be able to use this knowledge in a number of ways. For example, they think it will become possible to create a new source of clean, cheap renewable energy."

"But who doesn't want that?" cried George.

"I have hacked into their secret membership files," Reeper explained, "so I am one of the very few people who can actually identify the leaders of TOERAG. It's made up first of big companies—who would prefer us to keep on using coal, oil, gas, or nuclear energy rather than look for sources of renewable energy. They think that experiments at the LHC might one day give us the clue as to how to produce clean, cheap energy and they don't want that."

"Urgh!" said George. "You mean the people who mess up the seas and poison the atmosphere with greenhouse gases?" He thought of his eco-activist parents and how they tried their hardest to protect the planet. They were just normal, ordinary, kind people who wanted to make a difference to the future of the life on Earth. What chance did they have against such powerful opponents?

"Not just them," warned Reeper. "There's also a group within TOERAG who think that once we find one unified theory for the four forces, it will result in the elimination of war. They think that we will come to understand that we are all the same, all part of the same human race. This could raise our awareness of the problems on planet Earth, end competition for resources, and make the rich countries want to help the poor nations."

"Don't they want peace?" George was bewildered.

"No," said Reeper shortly. "They make a lot of

money selling weapons so that people can kill each other. They'd really prefer it if we kept waging war."

"Anyone else?" said George.

"Well, there are a few astrologers who think their predictions will become worthless once Eric and the other scientists can explain everything. So they won't be able to make money by telling your fortune on the Internet. There's a television evangelist who fears that no one will want to be saved by him if Eric is successful. Another group has joined out of fear—fear of science and what it will do in the future. There are even some scientists."

"Scientists?" said George in shock. "Why would they join TOERAG?"

"Well, there's me, for a start," said Reeper. "I didn't really join—I infiltrated TOERAG in order to spy on them. I heard about this secret, anti-science organization, and so to find out more, I became one of their number—my codename is *Isaac*, after one of the greatest scientists of all, Isaac Newton. In order to gain acceptance, I lied and told them that Eric and I were still sworn enemies. No one yet knows that he and I made peace with each other, so they believed me and let me in."

"Does Eric know you are part of TOERAG?" asked George.

"No," admitted Reeper. "I wish he did. I wanted to talk to him about their plans, but I realized it would put him in even more danger if I contacted him directly."

"Who are the other scientists?"

"That's more difficult," said Reeper. "We're never allowed to meet each other. We have separate jobs to do and our paths never cross."

"What was your job?"

"My job"—there was a trace of pride in Reeper's voice—"was to create a bomb, a really powerful and intelligent one. They wanted me to make a bomb that would be impossible to defuse. The thing about most bombs is that you can cut the wires to stop  them detonating. TOERAG wanted a bomb that even if you snipped the wires or knew the code, you still couldn't prevent the explosion. They said," Reeper added hastily, "it was just a prototype, for experimental purposes only."

"You didn't really do it, did you?" asked George. "I mean, you didn't actually make a bomb that works and give it to a dangerous underground anti-science group?"

"Of course I did!" said Reeper, sounding startled. "How could I make something that didn't work?"

"Duh, quite easily!" said George. "Then it wouldn't be able to blow anything up. Problem solved!"

"But I'm a scientist!" bleated Reeper. "I can't make something that doesn't work! I have to get it right—otherwise I'm not a scientist! And that would be . . ." He trailed off.

"You'd better tell me about this bomb," George said, trying to be patient.

"Right, well," said Reeper, sounding more enthusiastic. "It's really brilliant! And it can blow up anything—I mean, just anything!"

"Yup, I got that," said George. "You keep on telling me."

"Sorry, sorry!" said Reeper. "Okay, I designed a bomb with eight switches. You input a code on a numerical pad to make the switches go live. Then, when you push all eight of the switches, it creates a superposition of eight states. Once all eight switches are thrown, the countdown automatically begins."

"So what is the really super-clever part?" asked George.

"Because it's a quantum mechanical bomb"—Reeper sounded like he was boasting, just a little—"it has created a quantum superposition of the different alternatives inside the detonator. This means that anyone who tries to defuse the bomb by cutting one of the cables or flipping one of the switches would just blow themselves and everyone else up. That's the point—they wanted a bomb that couldn't be shut down, in case there were traitors inside TOERAG."

"I don't get it," said George.

"The bomb has been armed in such a way that no one switch can turn it off; it is in a quantum superposition of eight different possible switches. The detonator does not 'decide' which switch is actually being used until someone presses one to try to stop the bomb going off, and the circuit checks whether it is correct. At that point the wave function collapses randomly to one of the eight possible alternatives. Even if you pressed all eight at once, the bomb will very probably detonate immediately. What I mean is—it will explode, no matter what you do to it."

"Why did you do this?" asked George grimly.

"Because I wanted someone to know how clever I am," said Reeper sulkily. "I didn't realize they actually intended to use the wretched thing. They said it was just an experiment."

"And where is this impossible-to-defuse quantum mechanical bomb?"

"Well, I don't know!" said Reeper, sounding panicky. "That's the problem—it's gone!"

"Gone where?"

"They've taken it away. And from what I've learned by hacking into their computers, it looks like they mean to use it, after all. Where's Eric?"

"He's at the Large Hadron Collider...," said George slowly as the true horror of the situation became clear to him. "At a meeting of the Order of Science to Benefit

Humanity. Every single full-member of the Order will be there. They've been asked to come together."

"That's it!" cried Reeper. "That's where they are going to use the bomb! They're going to use it to destroy the Collider, and not just Eric, but all the leading physicists in the world!"

"But . . . but . . . but how could they know that the Order of Science is having a meeting?" gasped George.

"I have long suspected that the Order contains a mole," said Reeper, speaking quickly now. "One of the scientists in TOERAG must also be a member of the Order of Science. He or she must have betrayed the Order to TOERAG."

"And that person definitely isn't you?" asked George fiercely.

"I'm not even a member of the Order," said Reeper sadly. "So it couldn't be me. My membership was revoked many years ago and I was not allowed to rejoin. It is someone else, someone really dangerous."

"Why are you trying to help Eric now?" wondered George.

"George," said Reeper, "I know you don't have a high opinion of me. But believe me, what I love above all else is science. I can't just stand by and, after all these centuries of work, see it extinguished by idiots who are acting out of greed or prejudice. I joined TOERAG to try to stop them. That's why I'm here."

George's head was spinning. Could Reeper really

PARTICLE COLLISIONS

If there were no forces, particles colliding inside machines like the LHC would come out the same as they went in. Forces allow fundamental particles to influence each other in collisions (even to change into different particles!) by emitting and absorbing special force-carrying particles called *gauge bosons*.

Physicists can represent a collision by using **Feynman diagrams**. Such diagrams show the ways in which it is possible for particles to scatter off each other. One Feynman diagram is one part of describing such a collision and the diagrams need to be summed up for a complete description of a single collision.

Here is the simplest kind, in which two electrons approach, exchange a single photon, and then continue on their way. Time goes from left to right, the wiggly line is a photon, and the solid lines show the electrons (marked as e). This diagram includes all the cases where the photon travels up to down or down to up (which is why the wiggly line is drawn vertically):

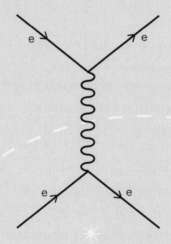

More complicated processes have more than one virtual particle in more complex Feynman diagrams. For example, here is one with two virtual photons and two virtual electrons:

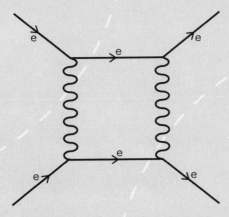

An infinite number of many diagrams are needed to fully describe each kind of particle reaction, though thankfully scientists can often obtain very good approximations by only using the simplest ones. Here's one that could represent what might happen at the Large Hadron Collider when protons collide! The letters u, d, and b are quarks; while g shows gluons:

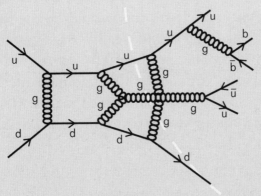

be telling the truth? If so, this would be the first time he wasn't concealing some deadly trick, intended to exterminate Eric and even up the score. He looked over at Reeper . . . but something had happened to him while George was absorbed in his thoughts. He seemed to be fading, disappearing into the blackness of the Andromeda galaxy around him.

"George," said Reeper urgently. "We have less time than I thought."

"What's happening to you?"

"I'm not real." Reeper was talking very fast now. George could no longer see his outline—only small triangles of reflected starlight on his shiny helmet and boots. "I am a computer-generated avatar of myself. It was the only way I could meet you. When I couldn't find Pooky or Eric or Cosmos, I broke into your house and secretly left a re-router downstairs. Through that re-router, I used Pooky to send myself here and open the portal remotely to transport you."

"Why don't you avatar *yourself* to the Collider and tell them?" cried George. "Why *me*?"

"I cannot get to the Collider!" said Reeper, his voice distorting. "I will not be able to escape them again."

"What about the quantum mechanical bomb?" cried George.

"There's a way! I'm not a complete fool! I made an observation! Pooky sent you a code . . ."

"What! How do I use Pooky's code? How do I defuse the bomb?"

But the only reply George got was a faint whisper through his voice transmitter: "George . . ."

And with that, the Universe around him fell silent. In front of him, where Reeper had stood, the silvery tunnel had opened up once more, pulling him forward into its river of light.

He twisted and turned at unimaginable speed across

the Universe, flying quintillions of miles from Andromeda back to our own Galaxy, the Milky Way, which is made up of matter and dark matter—that mysterious dark substance that surrounds us but which we can't see, feel, or hear. As he traveled, a thought flew into his brain—*I have been to the dark side*, he said to himself. *I have been to the dark.*

THE DARK SIDE OF THE UNIVERSE

One of the simplest questions we can ask is: What is the world made of?

Long ago, the Greek Democritus postulated that everything is made of indivisible building blocks he called *atoms*. And he was right—and over the past two thousand years we have filled in the details.

All the stuff in our everyday world is made of combinations of the ninety-two different types of atoms: the elements of the periodic table—hydrogen, helium, lithium, beryllium, boron, carbon, nitrogen, oxygen, and all the way up to uranium, number ninety-two. Plants, animals, rocks, minerals, the air we breathe, and everything on Earth is made of these ninety-two building blocks. We also know that our Sun, the other planets in our Solar System, and other stars far away are made of the same ninety-two chemical elements. We understand atoms very well, and are masters at rearranging them into all kinds of different things, including my favorite, French fries! The science of chemistry is all about building different things with atoms, a kind of "Lego with atoms."

Today, we know there is a whole lot more out there than just our Solar System—a mindbogglingly large Universe, with billions of galaxies, each made of billions of stars and planets. So what is the Universe made of? Surprise—while our Solar System and other stars and planets are made of atoms, most of the stuff in the Universe is *not*; it is made of very strange stuff—dark matter and dark energy—that we do not understand as well as atoms.

First the numbers: In the Universe as a whole, atoms account for 4.5%, dark matter for 22.5%, while dark energy comes in at 73%. An aside: Only about one in ten of those atoms is in the form of stars, planets, or living things, with the rest existing in a gaseous form too hot to have made stars and planets.

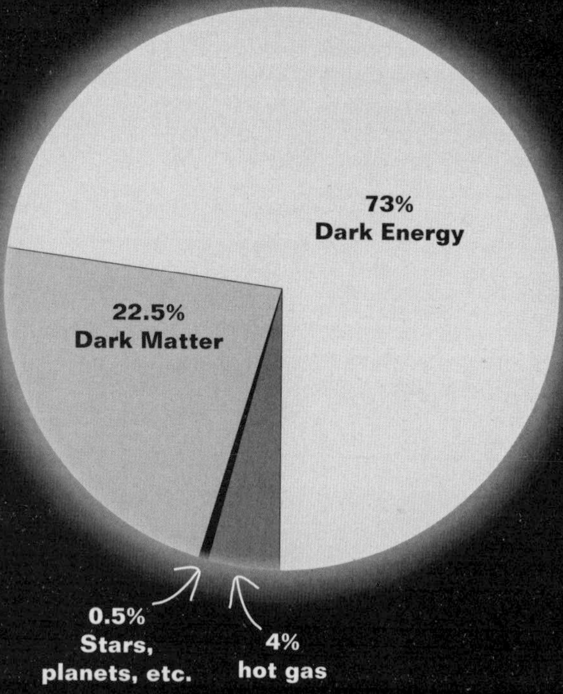

73%
Dark Energy

22.5%
Dark Matter

0.5%
Stars,
planets, etc.

4%
hot gas

Let's begin with dark matter. How do we know it is there? What is it? And how come we don't find it on Earth or even in our Sun?

We know it is there because the force of its gravity holds together our Galaxy, the Andromeda galaxy, and all the other big structures in the Universe. The visible part of the Andromeda galaxy (and all other galaxies) sits in the middle of an enormous (ten times larger) sphere of dark matter (astronomers call it the dark halo). Without the gravity of the dark matter, most of the stars, solar systems, and everything else in galaxies would go flying off into space, which would be a very bad thing.

At the moment we don't know exactly what the dark matter is made of (not unlike Democritus, who had an idea—atoms—but didn't have the details). But here is what we *do* know.

Dark matter particles are not made of the same parts that atoms are (protons, neutrons, and electrons); it is a new form of matter! Don't be too surprised—it took nearly two hundred years to identify all the different kinds of atoms, and over the course of time, many new forms of atomic matter were discovered.

Because dark matter is not made of the same pieces as atoms, it is pretty much oblivious to atoms (and vice versa). Moreover, dark matter particles are oblivious to other dark matter particles. A physicist would say that dark matter particles interact with atoms and with themselves very weakly, if at all. Because of this fact, when our Galaxy and other galaxies formed, the dark matter remained in the very large and diffuse dark matter halo, while the atoms collided with one another and sank to the center of the dark halo, eventually forming stars and planets made almost completely of atoms.

The "shyness" of dark matter particles, then, is why stars, planets, and we are made of atoms and not of dark matter.

Nonetheless, dark matter particles are buzzing around our neighborhood—at any given time there is about one dark matter particle in a good-sized tea cup. And this is key to testing this bold idea. Dark matter particles are shy, but can occasionally leave a telltale signature in a very, very sensitive particle detector. For this reason, physicists have built large detectors and placed them underground (to shield them from the cosmic rays that bombard the surface of the Earth) to see if dark matter particles really do comprise our halo.

Even more exciting is creating new dark matter particles at a particle accelerator by turning energy into mass, according to Einstein's famous formula, $E = mc^2$.

The Large Hadron Collider in Geneva, Switzerland, the most powerful particle accelerator ever built, is trying to create and detect dark matter particles.

And satellites in the sky are looking for pieces of atoms that are created when dark matter particles in the halo occasionally collide and produce ordinary matter (the reverse of what particle accelerators are trying to do).

If one or more of these methods are successful—and I hope that at least one will be—we will be able to confirm that something other than atoms makes up the bulk of the matter in the Universe. Wow!

And now we are ready to talk about the biggest mystery in all science: *dark energy*. This is such a big puzzle that I am confident it will be around for one of you to solve. Solving it might even topple Einstein's theory of gravity, General Relativity!

We all know that the Universe is expanding, having grown in size for the past 13.7 billion years after the Big Bang. Since Edwin Hubble discovered the expansion more than eighty years ago, astronomers have been trying to measure the slowing of the expansion due to gravity. Gravity is the force that holds us to the Earth, keeps all the planets orbiting the Sun, and is generally nature's cosmic glue. Gravity is an attractive force—it pulls things together, slows down balls and rockets that are launched from Earth—and so the expansion of Universe should be slowing down due to all the stuff attracting all the other stuff.

In 1998 astronomers discovered that this simple but very logical idea couldn't be more *wrong*; they discovered that the expansion of the Universe is not slowing down, but instead it is *speeding up*. (They did this by using the time-machine aspect of telescopes: Because light takes time to travel from across the Universe to us, when we look at distant objects we see them as they were long ago. Using powerful telescopes—including the Hubble Space Telescope—they were able to determine that the Universe was expanding more slowly long ago.)

How can this be? According to Einstein's theory, some stuff—stuff even weirder than dark matter—has repulsive gravity. *Repulsive gravity* means gravity that pushes things apart rather than pulling them together, which is very strange indeed!) It goes by the name of *dark energy* and could be something as simple as the energy of quantum nothingness or as weird as the influence of additional space-time dimensions! Or there may be no dark energy at all, and we need to replace Einstein's Theory of General Relativity with something better.

Part of what makes dark energy such an important puzzle is the fact that it holds the fate of the Universe in its hands. Right now, dark energy is stepping on the gas pedal and the Universe is speeding up, suggesting that it will expand forever, with the sky returning to darkness in about one hundred billion years.

Since we don't understand dark energy, we can't rule out the possibility that it will put its foot on the brake at some time in the future, perhaps even causing the Universe to recollapse.

These are all challenges for the scientists of the future—you, maybe?—to explore and understand.

Michael

Chapter Thirteen

Eric was standing in the main control room at the LHC, in front of the CCTV screens that showed ATLAS, 100 meters (328 feet) below in its cave, one of the gargantuan detectors at the Large Hadron Collider. ATLAS was the largest of its kind ever built, a colossal piece of engineering that dwarfed the tiny human beings who had created its mighty bulk. But entry to the mile-long tunnels housing the accelerator, and the huge man-made caves housing ATLAS and the other detectors, was now forbidden, and all the doors were sealed. No one was allowed into that part of the underground complex while the LHC was running.

According to the official schedule, the start of the great experiment—complete with politicians pressing a red button—was still weeks away. This was meant to be the dress rehearsal, a time when the scientists could work out whether they had thought of everything and could sort out their last technical problems before the experiment began for real. However, everything had gone so well that the trial run was now indistinguishable from the real thing. The proton beams were already circling in opposite directions through the tunnels more than eleven thousand times per second, creating six hundred million collisions per second, and ATLAS was reading the collision data.

The Large Hadron Collider (LHC)

CERN

CERN—properly known as the European Organization for Nuclear Research—is an international particle physics laboratory on the border of France and Switzerland.

In 1990 a CERN scientist, Tim Berners-Lee, invented the World Wide Web as a way of allowing particle physicists to share information easily—now the Web is an everyday tool for many people!

Founded in 1954, CERN has been operating colliders for more than fifty years now as part of its research into fundamental particles.

In 1983, the Super Proton Synchrotron (SPS) collided protons and antiprotons (the antimatter version of the proton) together and discovered the W and Z particles, which carry the weak nuclear force. The SPS is built inside a circular tunnel 7 kilometers (4.3 miles) in circumference, and today feeds protons to the LHC.

In 1988, after three years of digging, a new 27-kilometer (17-mile)-circumference circular tunnel 100 meters (328 feet) underground was completed to house the Large Electron-Positron collider (LEP). The LEP collided electrons with positrons (the antimatter version of the electron).

In 1998, work began on digging the detector caverns for the LHC. The LEP was turned off in November 2000 to make way for this new collider in the same tunnel.

The LHC was fully turned on for the first time in September 2008.

The Large Hadron Collider (LHC)

THE LHC

This is world's largest particle accelerator.

Two beam pipes run along the 27-kilometer (17-mile) circular tunnel of the LHC, each carrying a beam of protons, traveling in opposite directions. It's like a huge electromagnetic racetrack!

Inside the pipes, almost all the air has been pumped out to create a vacuum like there is in outer space, so that the protons can travel without hitting air molecules.

The core of the LHC is the most lifeless place on Earth!

Because the tunnel is curved, more than 1200 powerful magnets around the tunnel bend the protons' course so that they don't hit the walls of the pipe. The magnets are superconducting, which means they can generate very large fields with very little loss of energy. This requires them to be cooled with liquid helium down to -456 degrees Farenheit (-271 degrees Celsius)—colder than outer space!

All in all, there are around 9,300 magnets at the LHC.

At full power, each proton will perform 11,245 laps of the ring per second, traveling at more than *99.99% of the speed of light*. There will be up to six hundred million head-on collisions between protons per second.

As well as protons, the LHC is also designed to collide lead ions (nuclei of lead atoms).

THE GRID

With about one megabyte of data per collision, the LHC detectors produce too much data for even the most modern storage equipment. Computer algorithms select only the most interesting collision events—the rest, more than 99% of the data, are discarded.

Even so, the data from collisions at the LHC in one year is expected to be fifteen million gigabytes (which would fill seventeen thousand PCs with a two-hundred-gigabyte hard drive each). This creates a massive storage and processing problem, especially since the physicists who need the data are based all over the world.

The storage and processing is shared by sending the data rapidly over the Internet to computers in other countries. These computers, together with the computers at CERN, form the worldwide *LHC Computing Grid*.

The Large Hadron Collider (LHC)

The Detectors

The LHC has four main detectors situated in underground caverns at different points around the circumference of the tunnel. Special magnets are used to make the two beams collide at each of the four points along the ring where the detector caverns are situated.

ATLAS is the biggest particle detector ever built. It is 46 meters (151 feet) long, 25 meters (82 feet) high, 25 meters (82 feet) wide, and weighs 7,000 metric tons (15,432,359 pounds). It will identify the particles produced in high-energy collisions by tracing their flight through the detector and recording their energy.

CMS (Compact Muon Solenoid) uses a different design to study similar processes to ATLAS (having two different designs of detector helps to confirm any discoveries). It is 21 meters (69 feet) long, 15 meters (49 feet) wide, and 15 meters (49 feet) high, but weighs more than ATLAS at 14,000 metric tons (30,864,716 pounds).

ALICE (A Large Ion Collider Experiment) is designed specifically to search for quark-gluon plasma produced by colliding lead ions. This plasma is believed to have existed very soon after the Big Bang. ALICE is 26 meters (85 feet) long, 16 meters (52 feet) wide, 16 meters (52 feet) high, and weighs about 10,000 metric tons (22,046,226 pounds).

LHCb (Large Hadron Collider-beauty)—the "beauty" in the name of this experiment refers to the beauty, or *b* quark, which it is designed to study. The aim is to clarify the difference between matter and antimatter. It is 21 meters (69 feet) long, 10 meters (33 feet) high, 13 meters (43 feet) wide, and weighs 5,600 metric tons (12,345,886 pounds).

50m —
40m —
30m —
20m —
10m —
0m —

46 meters — Length
25 meters — Width
25 meters — Height

ATLAS
7,000
metric tons

21 meters — Length
15 meters — Width
15 meters — Height

CMS
14,000
metric tons

26 meters — Length
16 meters — Width
16 meters — Height

ALICE
10,000
metric tons

21 meters — Length
13 meters — Width
10 meters — Height

LHCb
5,600
metric tons

The Large Hadron Collider (LHC)

New Discoveries?

The Standard Model of particle physics describes the fundamental forces, the particles that transmit those forces, and three generations of matter particles.

But . . .

Only 4.6% of the Universe is made from the type of matter we know. What is the rest made of (the dark matter and dark energy)?

Why do elementary particles have masses? The Higgs boson—a particle predicted by the Standard Model but never observed—could explain this. Hopefully the LHC will see the Higgs for the first time.

Why does the Universe contain so much more matter than antimatter?

For a brief time, just after the Big Bang, quarks and gluons were so hot that they couldn't yet combine to form protons and neutrons—the Universe was filled with a strange state of matter called quark-gluon plasma. The LHC will re-create this plasma, and the ALICE experiment is set to detect and study it. In this way, scientists hope to learn more about the strong nuclear force and the development of the Universe.

New theories are trying to bring gravity (and space and time) into the same quantum theory that already describes the other forces and subatomic particles. Some of these ideas suggest there may be more than the familiar four dimensions of space-time. Collisions at the LHC could allow us to see these "extra dimensions," if they exist!

Even though the smooth running of the great experiment should have been a source of great happiness for Eric, instead it was a lonely and strange time. His colleagues and friends were sympathetic but distant. Until the Order resolved the dark cloud hanging over his name, Eric was a controversial figure whom people tended politely to avoid.

Even worse than the isolation from his peers, Eric realized he was on the cusp of becoming alienated from his work. The round of experiments being prepared were the most powerful of all, and might unlock the answers to the great questions of physics. But, Eric suddenly realized, if the meeting went against him and he was thrown out of the Order of Science, he would have to leave immediately; he might not be here to witness the most important moment in science since the Big Bang. No matter what the results of the experiment, Eric realized he might be banned from reading the data. Until he was reinstated as a trusted and responsible colleague, he remained a solitary and suspect individual, on the fringes of the scientific world. Was this, he wondered, what he himself had done to Dr. Reeper all those years ago? Was this how Reeper had felt when he found himself reviled and rejected by all his peers? Eric sank in gloom as he considered his future, spent far away from the work he loved above all else.

His pager beeped.

Meeting confirmed tonight at 19.30 hrs. Underground

trigger room, read the flashing letters. Eric gulped. At last, his fate would be decided.

Eric had been waiting for some time now. It had taken all the members of the Order of Science longer to get here than they had at first calculated. Eric didn't even have Cosmos for company. The supercomputer had been confiscated the minute he had stepped onto the tarmac in Switzerland from his small jet. Dr. Ling, the Chinese scientist who had spotted Eric and George on the Moon, had been waiting for him at the airfield.

"I'm so sorry, Eric," Dr. Ling had said, looking very embarrassed, unable to meet Eric's eye as the rain poured down from the night sky, "but you must hand Cosmos over immediately."

"What will happen to him?" asked Eric.

"He will be interviewed by The Grid," said Dr. Ling. "The Grid will review all Cosmos's activities since he was put in your care."

An image of Freddy flashed into Eric's mind. He wondered what The Grid, the vast and sprawling computer network that analyzed data from the Large Hadron Collider, would make of Cosmos and Eric transporting a pig from a farmyard to a peaceful rural setting. And of Eric and George's recent trip to the Moon—not to mention his various journeys around the Universe with not one but two kids in tow.

The Grid was one of the mightiest computers in the world, but he wasn't like Cosmos. Cosmos had a special power that The Grid completely lacked: He had empathy, and this allowed him to be creative, making him the world's most intelligent computer. Despite his name, The Grid was unable to bypass his own rigid rules or make intuitive connections between different pieces of information. In a straight contest, Eric knew clever little Cosmos would win every time against the enormous bully. But even so, Eric was sad to see his little silver friend taken away for such a challenging experience.

As he waited in the main control room Eric looked at the clock. Not long to go now until the meeting to decide his fate. He was still baffled by the speed at which his life had unraveled. Was it really so drastic, that photo taken on the Moon? Did it really merit this extraordinary meeting of the Order? Weren't they making a very big mountain out of what was, after all, just a lunar molehill?

A scientist walked past him, nose in the air, attempting to evade Eric's gaze.

Eric stopped him. "Is Professor Zuzubin here?" he asked anxiously. Perhaps he could persuade his old tutor to take a relaxed view of the incident. Maybe Zuzubin would ask the Order to go easy on Eric, provided he promised never to do anything like this again . . . ?

"Zuzubin?" said the scientist. "He's gone."

"Gone?" said Eric in surprise. "But I thought he called this meeting! Why wouldn't he stay when the result must be so important to him?" The other scientist didn't hang around to answer him, so Eric was left alone with his thoughts once more.

Something was very wrong here. The meeting had been arranged too quickly and on too flimsy an excuse. Zuzubin, who'd seemed to be in charge, had suddenly vanished, and Cosmos was now handcuffed to The Grid, being examined circuit by circuit. This, Eric suddenly realized, was not the way things should be. Something was very wrong indeed. But what could he do?

He looked at his cell phone. The screen was blank. Even here in the main control room, the Grid exerted a powerful blocking signal, meaning you could only use the internal paging system or the LHC phone network. Anyway, he realized with a shock, he didn't have anyone to call. The only person who would unquestioningly believe him was George, and this really wasn't the moment to bring a kid into this difficult and uncomfortable situation.

Sighing, Eric felt he might as well switch off his phone before the battery died. He mooched around the control room for a few more minutes but suddenly felt he couldn't stand it any longer. There was only one thing for it. Faced with the hostility and suspicion of his peers, bored of his isolation and lack of activity, and frustrated at the manner in which his opinion was being disregarded, Eric decided he would go for a long, soothing walk.

Chapter Fourteen

George shot out of the silver tunnel and landed on his belly, skidding across his bedroom floor. He lay there, panting, until he realized that, as on the asteroid, he was not alone. This time, two pairs of feet in sneakers were waiting for him. He rolled over onto his back. Through the window of his space helmet, two blurred faces peered down at him, distorted by the curved glass. One was fringed with blonde hair and had round, worried blue eyes. The other, topped by a plume of black spikes, looked totally astonished.

"George" — the smaller figure shook him — "you're back! You shouldn't have gone by your-self!"

Who were these people? George struggled to place them. It was as if they'd met once, in a strange dream, and he could no longer remember why or how he knew them. Lights danced in front of his eyes as he battled with the shifting, multi-colored cloud inside his head to form thoughts that meant something. But they just seemed to evaporate into the mist in his brain before he could seize on any of them to make sense of what was happening to him.

The taller figure grabbed George's hands in their space gloves and pulled him to his feet. But George couldn't stand up. It was as though his bones had melted and his muscles turned to mush.

"Oh, man!" the larger figure said, catching George as he crumpled to the floor. George's vision went in and out of focus, the swirling silver light of the tunnel still turning before his eyes. "Where did you come from? *What* was *that*?"

Looking around blearily, George could just about see that the portal had closed again and Pooky was still and quiet. Only these two facts seemed to signify anything to his confused mind. This strange person had him in his arms now, half-carrying him to the bed, where he laid George down, still wearing his space suit and perched uncomfortably on top of his oxygen tank. A pair of hands undid the clasp on his space helmet and took it off, then mopped George's soaking face with a corner of the duvet cover.

"Water!" shouted the smaller figure. "Get him some water!"

The other person dashed out of the room, coming back with a mug in his hands. "Here, drink this." He dribbled a few drops into George's mouth.

The small person was tugging off George's space boots. "George! It's me—Annie. Vincent, help me!" she ordered. "We need to get him out of this space suit."

They each took a boot, unclipped the fasteners, and pulled, both flying backward with a thump as they suddenly released George's feet from the heavy boots. But this didn't stop them for a second—they just got up and rushed back over to George, who was looking worse by the minute. His face was white as a sheet, except for his cheeks, which were mottled with bright pink patches, and his eyes rolled around

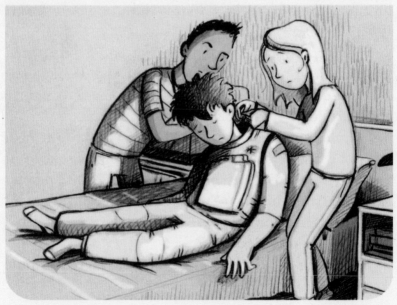

in their sockets as he tried and failed to focus them.

"What's happened to him?" cried Vincent as Annie sat George upright and unsnapped the oxygen tank from his back.

"Unzip him," she commanded.

Vincent unzipped the suit and dragged George's arms out of it. "Stand up," he said, lifting George up so that he could pull off the space suit, revealing George's shirt and jeans underneath.

George just flopped into Vincent's arms, as though he had no bones in his body. Vincent laid him carefully back down on the bed, using a T-shirt he found on the floor to wipe George's face, which was again covered in beads of sweat.

"The suit!" shouted Annie. "Give me the suit!" Vincent threw the heavy suit over to her and she started rifling through the pockets. "Where is it?" she muttered.

"He doesn't look so good," warned Vincent. "Shall I call a doctor?"

Annie looked up from the suit. "And say what?" she asked desperately. "*Our friend got back from space and he's not feeling well*? How can we explain that he traveled through an unauthorized portal that clearly wasn't safe?" Her voice was rising hysterically. Some green drool was now snaking out of George's mouth and dribbling down his chin.

"Help me!" said Annie. "Help me find the emergency space drops—they're in one of these pockets."

Vincent slid off the bed and grabbed the other half of the suit, which he patted all over, trying to feel for something in its depths. "Is this it?" He'd located a small plastic bottle in an arm pocket. SPACE RESCUE REMEDY it said in cheery red letters on the bottle. Vincent read out the words on the label. "*Do you need a space rescue? Have you had a bad space experience? Nausea? Loss of vision? Muscles turned to glue? Hair loss?*" He looked anxiously at George, who still seemed to have a full head of hair.

"Give!" shouted Annie.

"Have you taken this before?" said Vincent suspiciously, holding onto the bottle.

"Never needed to," she admitted. "But Dad always told us to take it if we were travel-sick after a space journey."

"Where does it come from?" said Vincent.

"We get it from Space Adventures R Us. They send it with each space suit my dad buys," said Annie. "But I never imagined we'd actually use it."

Vincent tossed it over to her and noticed that George was now twitching violently. Annie gently squirted a few drops from the nozzle of the small bottle into George's mouth. Some of the amber liquid oozed out between his numb lips, which were now turning blue.

"Please, planets and stars," muttered Annie, "make

this work for George!" She carefully squirted a few more drops into his mouth.

"Did you check the dose?" Vincent asked her.

"It's okay," she said. "The bottle only contains one dose, so you can't take too much; that's what Dad said."

As she spoke, George's lips started turning pink again, and his face was changing from mottled white and pink to its usual healthy color. His breathing slowed from rapid gasps to a gentle whoosh, and his eyelids fluttered as the Space Rescue Remedy ran though his system, putting right the things the cosmic journey had messed up.

"Oh, George!" said Annie—and burst into tears. Vincent came over to give her a hug—just as George's eyes opened again.

"What the . . . ?" mumbled George.

Annie and Vincent sprang apart and rushed over to either side of the bed.

"George! You're alive!" Annie kissed him sloppily on the cheek.

George's head was pounding. "Annie . . . ?" he mumbled. "Is that you?"

"It's me!" she said joyfully. "And Vincent," she added. "We saved you! You came through some weird-looking tunnel in your space suit and started having a fit."

"I had a fit?" repeated George, who was feeling stronger by the second. He sat up and looked around his bedroom.

"You were dribbling," said Vincent helpfully. "And your eyes had gone crazy."

George lay back down on the bed and let his eyelids close. This was all super-weird. He tried to remember what had happened, but the only image he could focus on was Annie hugging Vincent when he'd come out of his brightly colored delirium.

"George," she said urgently. "Where were you? What were you doing, out in space without us?"

"*Us?*"

"Me and Vincent," said Annie, a touch impatiently now that she could see George was going to be fine. "We would have come with you, if you'd just waited. We got here as quickly as we could, once you stopped talking on the phone."

"How did you get in the house?" George's brain had not yet recovered enough to take him back to space—it could only deal with the details of what was going on immediately around him.

A wail from downstairs answered the question. "Your mom and the twins," said Annie. "Daisy let us in."

"Does she know? About the space portal?" said George, sitting up again in panic.

"No, she's too busy with the babies—they make so much noise, I don't think she heard anything," said Annie.

"Here, drink this." Vincent handed George a mug of water.

George took a huge gulp and then nearly spat it out. "What is that?" he said in disgust.

"Sorry," said Vincent. "It's the toothbrush mug. It was the first thing that came to hand."

"C'mon," urged Annie. "C'mon, George, *think*! Where have you been? Why did you go?"

George's mind snapped into focus. It all came whooshing back to him, brilliantly clear and very, very urgent.

"Oh, holy supersymmetric strings . . . ," he said slowly, using Emmett the computer geek's favorite phrase. He looked at Annie and Vincent, deciding on what to say. "Vincent, can I trust you?"

"I think you have to," said Annie, putting her arm around George, "given what he's just seen. And he helped save your life. Just tell us, George—what happened to you out there?"

He thought for a second. There was more at stake here than just his feelings. He might not be super-fond of Vincent, but the karate kid was here now, and obviously he knew everything.

George took a deep breath. "I've seen Reeper," he told them.

"So he was there," said Annie, "waiting for you."

"That's the creepy guy, right?" said Vincent, reaching over and taking a swig out of George's toothbrush mug.

"Um—yeah," said George. "He took me out to an asteroid in Andromeda."

"Andromeda!" squeaked Annie. "Wow! I've never been that far." She almost sounded jealous.

"I wouldn't recommend it." George grimaced. "I don't think Pooky's portal would pass any safety checks."

"You looked rough, man," said Vincent admiringly.

"You must be made of strong stuff."

"Er, thanks," said George.

At that moment his mom knocked on the door and poked her head in. "I brought you some broccoli and spinach muffins!" She passed a plate into the room.

"Thanks, Mrs. G," said Annie, swiftly taking the plate and

blocking the doorway until Daisy had disappeared downstairs, summoned by another angry wail from one of the twins. "They look delicious!" Annie called after her.

Vincent, who was always hungry, fell on the plate of muffins with a little cry of joy. As he tasted them, his expression changed from delight to surprise.

"Oh my God!" he exclaimed through a mouthful of crumbs.

Annie kicked him sharply before he could make any rude comments about Daisy's cooking. It was all right for her and George to laugh about it, but suddenly she realized that it wasn't okay for Vincent to make fun of George's mom.

"I just meant this tastes like serious energy food," Vincent assured her. "Like we eat before a karate championship. That's all. No wonder George is a man of steel, if this is what he lives on."

"What time is it?" asked George.

Vincent checked his watch. "Five-o-six," he replied.

"Five! We haven't got long! Hold on—what time is it in Switzerland?"

"Six-o-six," said Vincent.

"Right, we have to work fast," said George, speaking as quickly as he could. "Annie, you told me that the meeting of the Order is at seven thirty tonight. Reeper said that TOERAG has a bomb—a quantum mechanical bomb—and I bet they've primed it to go off when the meeting starts so that the Collider—and everyone near it—will be blown to kingdom come, and science will be set back by centuries."

"A quantum mechanical bomb?" said Annie, looking almost as sick as George had been a few minutes earlier. "What's *that*?"

"Well, I know what it *is*," confessed George, "but I'm not sure how to turn it off. We'd better take this with us." He picked up Pooky's string of numbers. "I'm not sure, but it might be the code to defuse the bomb. Or one of them, anyway."

"What makes you think Reeper is telling the truth?" demanded Annie.

"We can't know for sure, but I think he's on our side this time. And Eric's side. Reeper wants to stop the Collider and everyone around it from being blown up by those weirdos we saw in the cellar when we were looking for somewhere to put Freddy."

"How can you trust this Reeper guy?" threw in Vincent. "Hasn't he always double-crossed you in the past?"

Annie had pulled her cell phone out of her pocket. She tried calling her dad, but she couldn't get through. She couldn't even leave a message.

"I don't know if we can," said George. "We're taking a chance on him. But if we don't do something, it's likely that the Collider will explode during the meeting of the Order of Science this evening."

"How can we get there in time?" cried Annie. "We'd need to travel through a portal to do that, and we haven't got Cosmos!"

"There is another portal," said George, finally working it out in his head and discovering the missing link he had been searching for since his visit to the Math Department, "and I know where it is!"

"Where?" said Annie in confusion. "I thought Cosmos was the only supercomputer in the world — apart from Pooky, who isn't safe."

"You're right," agreed George. "We can't use Pooky again — we don't know how, and his portal is no good anyway. But we do know how to use *new* Cosmos, which means we might be able to operate *old* Cosmos."

"*Old* Cosmos . . . ?"

"Do you remember your dad's lecture?" George's brain was now working at the speed of light. "That crummy professor, Zuzubin, was there. He's the one who told Eric he had to go to Switzerland, and he's the one who called the emergency meeting of the Order of Science to Benefit Humanity."

"So what?" said Annie. "What are you saying?"

"When we left the Math Department, Zuzubin didn't

follow us," George continued. "He went down the stairs, instead of coming out."

"And . . . ?"

"Your dad once told us that when he was a student at Foxbridge, old Cosmos—the first supercomputer—lived in the basement of the Math Department. And after your dad's lecture, I saw Zuzubin go down the stairs to the basement when we were going out of the front door. *And* I saw him wearing a pair of yellow glasses, just like the ones Eric found when he fell into the black hole. Which means that someone has been traveling around the Universe, dropping stuff."

"And to do that, they must have a supercomputer," said Annie, catching on. "So you think that old Cosmos is in the basement of the Math Department and Zuzubin has been using him . . . ?"

"But Annie's dad was a student, like, zillions of years ago," Vincent pointed out. "Surely that computer's been shut down by now."

"That's what we're supposed to think," said George. "We're supposed to think that old Cosmos doesn't work. But if he does, and he can send Zuzubin to look at black holes, he could also send us to the Collider in time to defuse the quantum mechanical bomb."

"But why would Zuzubin keep a secret like that?" asked Annie.

"I don't know . . ." George's voice was full of foreboding. "But I think we're about to find out. We need

Looking back to the beginning of time with the LHC (Large Hadron Collider)—an international project based in Europe.

Two dramatically different views of the Whirlpool Galaxy.

The comparative sizes of our Milky Way galaxy (left) and an ultracompact galaxy in the early Universe (right). Both have the same number of stars!

he formative years of spiral galaxies—shown here by four barred spiral galaxies at varied distances om the Earth.

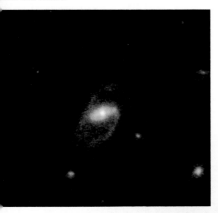

6.4 billion light-years

NASA, ESA, and Z. Levay (STScI)

5.3 billion light-years

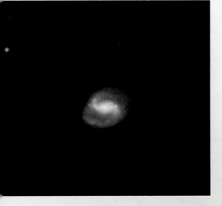

3.8 billion light-years

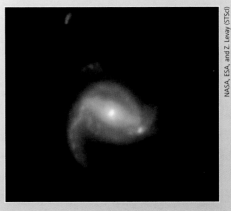

NASA, ESA, and Z. Levay (STScI)

2.1 billion light-years

Cosmic ice sculptures in the Carina Nebula . . .

A pillar of interstellar gas and dust within the Carina Nebula.

NASA, ESA, and M. Livio and the Hubble 20th Anniversary Team (STScI)

Above:
A visible-light view (different colors for different gases).

Right:
An infra-red view (colors assigned to different wavelengths).

to get to the Math Department. As fast as we can. Zuzubin will be at the Large Hadron Collider for the meeting, so we should be able to try old Cosmos."

He and Annie thumped down the stairs two at a time, sped out of the door, and got their bikes, with Vincent following closely behind. "What I don't get . . . ," Annie's friend said as he hopped onto his skateboard. "Why math? What has math got to do with anything? It's just a bunch of numbers on a blackboard that all add up to another number. What's that got to do with the Universe anyway? What use is math to anyone?"

HOW MATHEMATICS IS SURPRISINGLY USEFUL IN UNDERSTANDING THE UNIVERSE

It is obvious that some things in our everyday world are simple and others complex. We know our Sun will come up day after day exactly on time, but the weather changes in annoying and haphazard ways—unless like me you live in Arizona, where it is almost always warm and sunny. So you can set your alarm clock the night before and be sure you will wake up at the right time of day, but if you choose your clothes ahead of time you might get it badly wrong.

Those things that are simple, regular, and dependable can be described by *numbers*, like the number of hours in a day, or the number of days in a year. We can also use numbers to describe complicated things like the weather—such as the highest temperature each day—but in that case it's often hard to spot any patterns in the numbers.

Our ancestors noticed many patterns in nature: not just day and night, but the seasons, the movements of the Moon, stars, and planets in the sky, and the rise and fall of the tides. Sometimes they used numbers to describe the patterns; sometimes they used songs or poetry instead. Many ancient peoples went to a lot of effort with numbers and patterns to describe the movement of heavenly bodies. They liked to predict eclipses—scary but exciting events where the Moon blots out the light of the Sun and you can see the stars in the daytime. Knowing when an eclipse would happen required lots of boring calculations, and they didn't always get it right. But when they did, people were impressed.

Long ago, nobody knew why numbers and simple patterns occur so often in nature. But about four hundred years ago, some people began to study the patterns more carefully. Especially in Europe, there were beautiful and quite skillfully made instruments to help observe and measure things accurately. People had clocks and sundials and all sorts of metal gadgets for distances and angles and times. Eventually they had small telescopes, too. These curious people called themselves "natural philosophers"—and were what we would now call scientists.

One thing natural philosophers puzzled over was *motion*. At first, there seemed to be two sorts: stars and planets moving in the sky, and objects moving around on Earth. Everybody knows that when you throw a ball it travels in a curved path, and it doesn't take too many tries to see that the curve is always the same if the ball is thrown at the same speed and angle.

Of course, our ancestors were well aware that moving objects followed simple predictable paths. They knew it because their lives depended on it. Hunters needed to be sure that when a stone left a sling or an arrow left a bow, it would behave the same way today as it did yesterday. In Australia, the ancient people known as Aboriginals were so ingenious they could make a flat stick called a boomerang, and when it was thrown it would follow a special path that would cause it to curve back toward the thrower.

By the sixteenth century, mathematics had gone some way beyond simple arithmetic, to include algebra and other fancy methods, and the natural philosophers were able to write down equations to describe many of the patterns found in nature. In particular, they could write equations to describe curves like the paths of arrows and balls. For example, a simple equation describes a circle, a slightly different one a squashed circle called an ellipse, and yet another describes the curve of a rope hanging between two poles. Using this more advanced mathematics, a huge variety of patterns and shapes could be described not just in words, but in symbols and equations, written on paper and printed for other scientists and mathematicians to study.

Useful though all this was, it was still just a description of patterns in nature, not an explanation. The big breakthrough began with the work of Galileo Galilei in Italy in the early seventeenth century. Everybody knows that when an object is dropped from a height, it rushes toward the ground faster and faster. Galileo wanted to make this precise: How much faster does it go after one second, two seconds, three seconds . . . ? Was there a pattern? He found the answer by experimenting—he tried dropping things and timing them. He rolled balls down slopes so everything happened more slowly and easily. Then he sat down with all the measurements and did some arithmetic and algebra, until he found a single formula that correctly describes the way that all falling bodies *accelerate*; that is, go faster and faster as they fall.

Galileo's formula is pretty simple: If the object is

dropped from rest its speed increases in proportion to the time it has been falling. This means that when the object has been falling for two seconds it's going exactly twice as fast as it was at one second. And there's more. If the object is thrown from a height at an angle instead of just dropped, it will still fall in the same way but it will also move horizontally, and Galileo's formula says that the shape of the path the object follows is a *parabola*—one of the curves mathematicians already knew about from studying geometry.

The decisive step came when Isaac Newton in England worked out how objects like balls change their motion (that is, accelerate or decelerate) when they are pushed or pulled by forces. He wrote down a very simple equation to describe it.

In the case of Galileo's falling objects, the force concerned is, of course, *gravity*. We feel the force of gravity all the time. Newton suggested that the Earth pulls everything downward, toward its center, with a force proportional to the amount of matter the object contains (known as its mass). Newton's equation connecting force and acceleration then explained Galileo's formula for falling bodies.

But this was just the start. Newton also suggested that not just the Earth, but every object in the Universe—including the Sun, Moon, planets, stars, and even people—pull on every other object with a force of gravity that gets weaker with distance in a precise way, called an *inverse square*. That's a fancy way of saying that at *twice* the distance from the center of the Earth (or the Sun, or the Moon) the force is one-*quarter* as strong; at *three* times the distance it is one-*ninth*, and so on.

Using this formula plus his equation for how force and acceleration are related, Newton was able to do some cool mathematics (some of which he invented) to work out how planets and comets move around the Sun, pulled by the Sun's gravity. He also calculated how the Moon goes around the Earth. And the numbers all came out right! More than that, the *shapes* of the orbits were also correctly described by his calculations. For example, astronomers had measured that the orbits of the planets are ellipses, and the great Newton showed they *should* be—from his calculations! No wonder everybody thought he was a hero and a genius. The government was so pleased they put him in charge of printing all England's money.

The really important thing about Newton's work on motion and gravitation is deeper, however. He proposed that his formula for gravity and his equation for force and acceleration were *laws of nature*. That is, they should be the same everywhere in the Universe and at all times, and can never change—rather like God, whom Newton believed in. Before Newton, some people thought the motions of objects on Earth, like balls and boats and birds, had nothing to do with the motions of bodies in the sky, like the Moon and planets. Now we knew they all obeyed the same laws. While other scientists had *described* motion, Newton *explained* it in terms of mathematical laws.

In practical terms, this was a huge leap forward, because now anyone could sit in a chair and work out how such-and-such an object would move, without ever seeing it, or even leaving the room. For example, you can calculate where a cannonball will land if it is fired at a certain speed and angle. You can work out how fast it would need to go to fly off the Earth and never come back. Using Newton's simple equations, engineers can figure out exactly how to point a rocket to send a spacecraft to the Moon or Mars—before they even have the money to build the rocket.

All this made physics—the study of the basic laws of the Universe—a *predictive* science. Physicists could play with their equations and predict things that nobody knew before, like the existence of unknown planets. Uranus and Neptune were found after astronomers used Newton's laws to work out where in the sky they should be, and we now use those laws to predict the existence of planets going around other stars.

Very soon physicists began applying the same ideas to other forces, like electricity and magnetism, and sure enough, they were found to obey simple mathematical laws, too. Then atoms and their nuclei were studied, and they also can be explained in detail with mathematical formulas. So there are now quite a number of equations in physics textbooks.

Some physicists wonder whether it will go on like this forever, or whether all the laws and equations can be merged in some way, into some super-duper law that contains all the others. Quite a lot of smart people have peered at the equations to look for links, and a few have been found that turned out to be right.

A famous example was when James Clerk Maxwell, a Scottish physicist in the nineteenth century, found that the laws of electricity and magnetism could be joined, and when he had done that he solved the equations and discovered that the combined *electromagnetic* force could generate waves of electromagnetism. When he worked out the speed of the waves from his equations, he found it was the same as the speed of light. Bingo! Light must be an electromagnetic wave, he said.

The quest for a super-duper law combining *all* the forces goes on. It needs a really bright youngster to pull everything together.

When I was a schoolboy, I liked a pretty girl called Lindsay. One day I was doing a homework problem in physics. I had to calculate (that is, predict) what angle to throw a ball for it to go the maximum distance up a hill of a certain slope. Lindsay (who was studying liberal arts) sat opposite me in the school library, which was nice, although it made me a little nervous. She asked what I was doing, and when I described the problem she remarked in wonderment, "But how can you find out what a ball will do by writing things on a piece of paper?" At the time I thought this was a silly question. After all, this was my homework! But Lindsay had actually touched on a very deep issue. Why can we use simple mathematical laws to describe, and even predict, things that go on in the world around us? Where do the laws come from? That is, why does nature have laws at all? And even if for some reason there have to be laws of nature, why are they so simple (like the inverse square law of gravity)? We can imagine a universe with mathematical laws that are so subtle and complicated that even the brainiest human mathematician would be baffled.

Nobody knows why the Universe can be explained with simple mathematics, or why human brains are good enough to work it all out. Maybe we just got lucky? Some people think there is a Mathematician God who made the Universe that way. Scientists are not very interested in gods, though. Could it be that life will arise only if the Universe has simple mathematical laws, so nature *has* to be mathematical or we wouldn't be here arguing about it? Perhaps there are many universes, each with laws different from our own, and maybe some with no laws to speak of at all. These other universes may be devoid of scientists and mathematicians. Or maybe not.

To be honest, it's all a mystery, and most scientists think it's not part of their job to worry about it. They just take the mathematical laws of nature as a fact, and get on with their calculations.

I'm not one of them. I lie awake at night turning it all over in my mind. I'd like an answer. But whether or not there is a reason for the mathematical simplicity of the Universe, it's clear that physics and mathematics are deeply interwoven, and that we will always need people who can do experiments and people who can do mathematics. And they had better keep talking to each other!

Paul

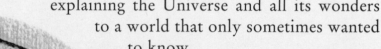

Chapter Fifteen

George and Annie pedaled furiously past Foxbridge's curiously shaped citadels of learning, Vincent curving gracefully beside them on his skateboard. The town was full of old and beautiful buildings, where for centuries scholars had dreamed up great theories, explaining the Universe and all its wonders to a world that only sometimes wanted to know.

Some of the colleges looked like fortresses—for good reason. Throughout the ages they had at times been forced to lock their gates to keep out angry mobs, furious at some of the new ideas their scholars had propounded. Gravity, for example. The orbit of the Earth around the Sun, rather than the other way around. Evolution. The Big Bang. The double helix of DNA, and the possibilities of life in other universes. The walls of these colleges were thick, with tiny windows to protect those within from a real and often unfriendly world outside.

The three children scooted into the court-yard of the Math Department,

throwing the bikes against the black railings and running up the steps to the front entrance. Today the glass doors just swung in the breeze, and no one stopped them as they dashed into the hallway. They were greeted only by the familiar smell of chalk dust and old socks, and by the distant clank of the tea tray being unloaded.

"Don't take the elevator!" hissed Annie as Vincent started to press the button. "It's too noisy! Let's go down the stairs."

Vincent parked his precious skateboard under the notice board in the hallway—he noticed ads for enticing events such as DOUBLY PERIODIC MONOPOLES: A 3D INTEGRABLE SYSTEM or THE EARLY UNIVERSE: TRANSITIONAL PHASES!—and the three of them tiptoed down the steps to the basement, George first, Annie next, and Vincent following behind.

When they reached the bottom of the stairs, they found that the dim lights in the basement were already on. They could just about see across the big room: It turned out to be full of junk—old office equipment, discarded computers, broken chairs, splintered desks, and reams and reams of computer paper. They picked their way cautiously through the terrible mess, guided by the sound of a computer whirring away somewhere behind the wall of debris. It soon became clear that they were not alone in the basement. Above the sound of the computer they heard a very clear and very human voice.

"No!" A howl of frustration. "Why, you stupid computer, won't you let me do what I want to do?"

Moving carefully forward—Annie and George in front, with Vincent, who was taller, poised behind them—they could see through the mess to where an old man in a tweed suit was attempting to operate an enormous computer. It stretched across one whole wall of the basement, such an antique that it was made up of compartments, what looked like cupboard doors, and great stacks of machinery, all piled on top of each other. In the middle was a monitor screen, on which the old man seemed to be watching a film. Only the top half of the set showed a picture—the bottom half had text scrolling across it in bright green letters on a black background.

"It's Professor Zuzubin," George whispered into Annie's ear. "He's here! He should be at the Collider— he said it was a meeting for all the Order of Science to Benefit Humanity and that means him as well."

"What's he doing?" asked Annie, speaking into George's ear in turn. They watched, agog, as Zuzubin ran the footage again in reverse, and the words scrolled backward off the bottom half of the screen. He pressed PLAY and the film started once more. As they watched the images, they could see a man who looked like a much younger version of Zuzubin himself, standing at the front of a packed auditorium in front of an old-fashioned overhead projector.

"It's the lecture hall where your dad gave his talk!" said George to Annie. "It's Zuzubin, and he's giving a lecture at Foxbridge!"

"He once had Dad's job," she murmured. "He was a math professor here."

"Maybe he wants his old job back," muttered George grimly; he didn't like the look of what he was seeing. "Look—in the audience! It's your dad!"

In the film, a young man with a thick shock of black hair, wonky glasses, and a big smile had just stood up.

"It *is* my dad!" said Annie, tears coming to her eyes. "Oh my God! I can't believe he was ever that young! What's he doing?"

Old Cosmos answered that question for them. "Professor Zuzubin," he said in a mechanical voice, speaking the words the young Eric was mouthing on the screen. "I have shown that your theory contains a flaw!" In typical Eric style, he looked as though

Zuzubin should be pleased by his remarks.

In the film, Zuzubin kept smiling, although his grin was becoming fixed onto his face as though stuck on with superglue.

Eric continued in the voice of old Cosmos: "I have shown that the model of the Universe that you propose violates the weak energy condition."

On the screen, Zuzubin's nostrils flared and he looked angry.

A singularity is a place where the mathematics used by physicists goes horribly wrong! For example, as you approach the center of a black hole—one type of singularity—space-time curvature grows to infinity and the normal rules of mathematics fail at the exact center (they say to divide by zero, which everyone knows isn't allowed!).

Sometimes a physics calculation makes an assumption that turns out to be wrong at a particular point, and a singularity is found. Once this is understood, the calculation can be adapted so that the error is fixed, the math works properly, and the singularity disappears. Good result!

The more interesting singularities are harder to get rid of and suggest that a new theory is needed. For example, black hole and Big Bang singularities occur in the math of General Relativity. Perhaps a theory with very different math is needed to understand what is really going on, and to get sensible results at such places in the Universe.

This is a busy area of research for scientists who hope that a Theory of Everything will get rid of these singularities.

The Big Bang

the space-time curvature becomes
infinite

the density of matter becomes
infinite

the temperature becomes
infinite

the space containing all we see around us
in the Universe reaches
zero size

and all paths going back in time come . . .
to an end.

This singularity is also known as an *initial singularity*
because it sits at the beginning of time.

"Bellis," recited old Cosmos, the words scrolling along on the text screen. "Your theories concerning this 'Big Bang' are interesting, but impossible to prove."

"I believe not!" said the young Eric. "The recently discovered microwave background radiation provides direct evidence in favor of the Big Bang model. Furthermore, I am firmly of the opinion that one day we will be able to build a great experiment that will show that the mathematical theories I have developed here at Foxbridge with my colleagues"—he gestured modestly to the people sitting around him—"are consistent with reality."

The real-life Zuzubin pressed PAUSE, and the picture froze. He frantically hammered the command buttons on Cosmos's keyboard. A little paintbrush appeared on the screen. Zuzubin swirled it around using a computer mouse he had attached to old Cosmos. The little paintbrush swept ineffectively over the picture, but nothing changed.

"Pah!" exclaimed Zuzubin. "Why won't this work!" he muttered to himself. "In that case, I shall try something else . . ."

He deleted all the text visible on the screen. Typing rapidly, he inserted the words: *Not so. The properties of the zuzon particle are the key to understanding the relationship between the four forces and the creation of matter. I predict that any experiment at the energy scale you propose will end in a dramatic and life-threatening explosion, which will prove that my theories about the nature of fundamental particles and the dynamics of the Universe are correct.*

But as soon as Zuzubin typed in the new text, the cursor moved back and erased it again, replacing it with the original speech.

"It's not a movie," murmured George. "It's the *past*! He's using Cosmos to view himself in the past, giving a lecture at Foxbridge! And he's trying to change it—it looks like he's made Cosmos some kind of Photoshop program to change what he said and did back then."

"Why?" asked Annie.

"He's trying to make it look like he predicted what's about to happen," said George. "He's using Cosmos to go back and change the past to make *his* theories look right—and your dad's wrong. And he's trying to show that he predicted that the Collider would explode."

Zuzubin had been too focused on what he was doing to notice any noise the kids might have made. But even he couldn't ignore the sound of George's cell phone bursting into song as the theme song from *Star Wars* rang through the basement.

George acted quickly. He dropped the phone on the floor, kicking it back toward Vincent, who knelt down to scoop it up, pressing END CALL and changing the ringtone to SILENT.

But it was too late. Zuzubin was on to them. Turning around, he glared—and then smiled as he saw two pairs of eyes staring back at him from the carefully arranged mountain of junk that he'd been using to hide the original supercomputer from the rest of the world.

"Ah, George!" he said, baring his teeth in a grin. "And look—my friend, little Annie. Come forward, my dear children. Come, come! Annie, I held you on my knee as a baby—you have nothing to fear from me!"

George and Annie had no choice. As they stepped forward, Vincent stayed down among the old furniture. Realizing that Zuzubin might not have spotted him, he figured that if he could hide in the basement, he might be able to  help Annie and George if they got into trouble. Vincent hadn't understood much of what the old scientist had said, but it was clear to him that anyone who was trying to change the past to make himself right and someone else wrong was not a person to be trusted.

"Annie," cooed Zuzubin. "So grown-up! So tall! So clever! How nice it is to see you again. But why so worried, children? Why so anxious? What can Professor Zuzubin do for you? Tell me, my dears. You can trust me!"

George pinched Annie to stop her speaking, but it

was no good. Annie was desperate enough to believe anyone who told her they could help.

"Professor Zuzubin . . . ," she said in a quavering voice.

The old man reached behind and surreptitiously turned off old Cosmos's monitor, so that the film of the past was no longer playing.

"We need to get to the Large Hadron Collider," Annie continued. "Something terrible is going to happen there! We must save my dad! We want you to send us to the LHC using old Cosmos, so that we get there in time to stop the bomb from going off."

"Your father is in trouble?" Zuzubin pretended to be concerned. "A bomb? The LHC? No, I don't believe it! Not Eric, surely . . ." He trailed off, viewing George with a suspicious eye.

"Don't say any more . . ." George was only whispering to Annie, but Zuzubin heard him.

"Whyever not?" he said. "Eric was my favorite pupil, my best ever success story. If he needs my help, then it would be my honor and privilege to provide it." He bowed low to show that this was indeed so.

Annie turned to George. "We don't have any other options," she said wildly. "There's no one else we can ask!"

"So you want to go to the Collider!" said Zuzubin smoothly. "Sure, that is no problem. You can be there in under a second." He entered a few commands on the keyboard, his hand hovering on a doorway into the great computer.

"When I open this door," Zuzubin purred, "Cosmos will take you directly to the place you need to be — directly to the right destination for you. You, Annie, can be the hero today. You, Annie, will solve all the problems and make everything good once more."

Annie's eyes sparkled. For once, *she* would be the hero. For once, *she* would be the person who made a difference, the one who saved the day. Not her dad, not her mom, not George. *Her.*

"I'll do it!" she said decisively. "Take me to the Collider!"

"Oh, but you can't travel alone," tutted Zuzubin, shaking his head. "Your little friend will have to travel with you. It must be you *and* George, or I cannot open Cosmos to transport you."

"Annie . . ." George tugged frantically at her T-shirt. "No! That doesn't make sense!"

"I don't care!" declared Annie. "Professor Zuzubin, open Cosmos and send us" — she turned and glared at George — "to the Collider."

"What about space suits?" said George desperately. "We haven't got them."

"You're not going into space," said Zuzubin in the same oily tone, "so why would you need them? This is just a short hop from one country to another. You step through the portal here"—his hand was on the doorknob—"and you will emerge almost instantly at your destination. I promise you this. I swear on my oath as a member of the Order of Science to Benefit Humanity that this is true."

"See?" said Annie. "He swore on the Oath—the one you took, the one I took—the one Dad and all his scientist friends took! He wouldn't lie, not about the Oath!"

"I most certainly would not," said Zuzubin gravely. "Now, Annie, listen carefully. You are the hero . . . you are going to travel through the portal . . . you are going to save the day." His voice had an oddly hypnotic quality. Annie blinked rapidly and her head seemed to sway around on her neck.

George looked at his watch. It was already six p.m. in Foxbridge, which meant it was seven p.m. in Switzerland—only thirty minutes until the quantum bomb went off, taking the great experiment, Eric, and all the world's top scientists with it. Zuzubin, sensing that George was weakening, winked at Annie and pulled the doorway open. Beyond it, they could see nothing—only darkness.

"Step through," said Zuzubin insistently. "Step through, dear children! Zuzubin will make sure you are safe and sound . . . safe and sound . . . nice dear little children."

As though in a trance, Annie stepped forward, sleep-walking into the dark doorway, through which she disappeared in a matter of seconds.

George couldn't let her go alone. He had no idea where she would end up: Even if some miracle *did* transport her to the Collider, she wouldn't be able to defuse the quantum mechanical bomb because she didn't have the code. He ran after her.

How different, he thought, the original Cosmos—the world's first ever supercomputer—was to new Cosmos, the sleek, personable, chatty little computer they had grown to know and love. Old Cosmos was like trying to steer a huge cruise liner when you were used to a sleek little speedboat.

Bracing himself, George stepped forward and passed once more through a portal to an unknown world of discovery and adventure, the darkness swallowing him whole.

Chapter Sixteen

From his vantage point among the junk, Vincent noted everything that happened. He watched Zuzubin's sinister face, and although he couldn't make out each word the old man said, he could see Annie looking conflicted and confused, and George turning red with anger. Vincent saw George protest but knew there was little the other boy could do.

Once Zuzubin opened the portal door, which Annie believed would lead them straight to the Collider and her father, Vincent—like George—knew their fate was sealed. He prepared himself to leap out of his hiding place. As always, before Vincent used his karate skills, he recited the karate mantra to himself:

"I come to you with only karate, empty hands. I have no weapons, but should I be forced to defend myself, my principles or my honor; should it be a matter of life or death, of right or wrong; then here are my weapons, karate, my empty hands."

But when Vincent looked up, Annie and George had disappeared, and only the old man Zuzubin was there in front of the great silent computer, laughing and laughing until the tears ran down his wrinkled cheeks and he had to bring out a perfectly pressed white hand-kerchief to wipe them away. When he finally stopped laughing, he switched the monitor back on, but this time he changed the channel.

Vincent peered through the debris to see what the old man was doing now—on the screen he could just make out the image of a room with two smallish figures moving around inside it. He edged closer, as quietly as he could, just as Zuzubin picked up an old-fashioned microphone and started speaking into it.

"George and Annie . . . ," he said.

On the other side of old Cosmos's doorway, George and Annie had stepped through and found themselves in complete darkness. Behind them, the portal door clicked shut. They had absolutely no idea where they were—until a light flipped on, illuminating their new surroundings. For a second, they just stood open-mouthed in surprise. They had never before stepped through a computer doorway and found themselves anywhere like this before. They were quite used to emerging from Cosmos's portal into different gravitational conditions, where they flew upward into the atmosphere of a strange planet, or got dragged down onto the surface. On their previous journeys, they'd stepped through Cosmos's portal to encounter lakes of dark methane, volcanoes that erupted in plumes of slow-moving, sticky lava, or planet-swallowing sandstorms. They'd seen a sunset with two suns in the sky as well as witnessing the fast-forwarded fate of an exploding black hole. But they'd never been anywhere like this before.

In some ways, it was just a room, so it was hard to say why it felt so creepy. It was square, the ceilings were of normal height, it had a comfy-looking sofa, a television set and a couple of cosy armchairs, a patterned rug on the floor, and bookshelves that held hundreds of hardcover books, their spines neatly arranged in alphabetical order.

On one of the armchairs, a cat stretched and purred. The curtains were closed, but Annie ran straight over to them and pulled them back. The two friends saw a view of a snow-capped mountain range, with dark fir trees on the lower slopes and a blue sky above the peaks, darker clouds gathering beyond the more

distant mountains. "Where are we?" Annie asked.

"I don't know," said George slowly, looking around. "But this is definitely not the Large Hadron Collider." They could both feel that something about this room was terribly, horribly wrong.

"Are those the Alps outside the window?" wondered Annie hopefully. "Should we open the door? Perhaps the Collider is nearby." The door they had come through had closed behind them. They both looked at it.

"Won't that just take us back to Foxbridge?" said George. "Don't we need another door to exit from wherever this is?"

At that moment the antique television set spontaneously crackled into life. Black and white flashes shot across the screen, showing only a small part of the fuzzy picture behind them. But the voice that addressed them was unmistakable. 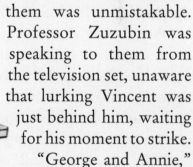 Professor Zuzubin was speaking to them from the television set, unaware that lurking Vincent was just behind him, waiting for his moment to strike.

"George and Annie," said the professor, his image settling onto the screen.

"It's *Zuzubin!*" screamed Annie. They could see

him clearly now, the collection of junk in the background as he loomed closer. Everything fell into place for George—the voices they had heard in the cellar, the yellow glasses Zuzubin had been wearing, the phrases he had heard on the radio news broadcast, the secret use of old Cosmos in the basement.

"It was *you* all along!" said George, speaking into the television set. "You've been traveling around the Universe, leaving things inside black holes! *You* invented the True Vacuum theory in order to scare ordinary people into joining TOERAG! *You* were the insider who betrayed the Order of Science. You set up the meeting tonight so that all the top physicists would be in one place—then you could blow them all up and be the only one left! You want to change what happened in the past to make it look like you were right all along—that your theories, which everyone has forgotten about, showed that the Large Hadron Collider would explode!"

"And," said Zuzubin nastily, "I have succeeded—in all my aims. In just a short while the Collider will indeed explode, and the world will realize that I am a scientist who should not have been forgotten! It will look like I was right all along and there will be no other physicists to contradict me. I have won!"

"No, you've cheated!" shouted George at the TV. "That's not winning—that's being the biggest loser of all."

Annie interrupted him. "Where *are* we?" she cried,

pressing her face against the screen. "You promised us we would arrive safely at the LHC! You swore on the Oath."

"Oh no, my dear," cackled Zuzubin. "If you listened more carefully and did not give in to your immature habit of making rash assumptions, you would have heard me correctly. I said you would arrive safely at your destination. Which you have. I never told you where that destination would be."

Annie ran over to the door and paused just in front of it.

"Wait!" said George. "Annie, don't open the door. We don't know what we'll find."

"Exactly," said Zuzubin. "You, my dear little friends, are in the Inverse Schrödinger Trap. It was so easy! You just walked straight in."

"What does that mean?" asked Annie in bewilderment.

"It means"—George gave a heavy sigh—"that we will only know where we are when we open the door. We could be anywhere at all, but we won't find out for sure while the door is still closed."

"Too good, too good," mused Zuzubin. "While the door remains closed, you are in an infinite number of locations. Shall I show you some of the possibilities?" The scene through the window changed to a vista of something glowing white-hot, with a yellowish tinge. Annie and George both recoiled from the glare coming through the window.

"Perhaps," said Zuzubin, "you are in the middle of planet Earth, held in the crystalline center of the inner core. In that case, you would be right in the heart of a one-and-a-half-thousand-mile ball of solid iron, which is about as hot as the surface of the Sun. The pressure is three point five million times the pressure on the surface of the planet. Open the door—please! Be my guest! I will be most intrigued to know what happens—will you fry or will you be crushed? Which will be first?"

George's jaw had dropped. He stared in horror at the window.

"Nothing to say for once?" said Zuzubin. "Then I will continue our lesson in geology. Around this iron ball lies an outer core of liquid iron—which, by the way, is exceedingly toasty as well—and around that, another mantle of rock through which volcanic lava sometimes escapes. Even if you did get that far, your blood would bubble in your veins, as it is unbelievably hot down there. But that isn't the end of it. From there, you'd have to dig through twenty-five miles of the rocky crust to get to the surface. Of course, after just a few miles, you might find that you'd broken through to the bottom of the ocean! Oh, children!" He clasped his hands together.

"Let's look at what that would be like for you!"

Annie sat down very suddenly on top of the cat, which yowled indignantly and wriggled out from under her to take up a position on the sofa, from where it shot her murderous looks as it washed its paws.

The picture through the window changed again. This time they were underwater in a deep trench, so far down that the sunlight never penetrated. In the light from the room behind them they could see squiggly reef formations and a plume of black smoke coming out of a hole in the ocean floor.

"Let's say you find yourself at the bottom of the Pacific, in a hot spring," gloated Zuzubin, "where strange prehistoric life-forms exist, hidden from human eyes, able to survive on the minerals expelled through the vents from the core of the Earth itself."

A massive worm, longer than either of the kids, swam straight at the window, bashing into it. Its long pallid body squelched along the glass as it retreated in surprise.

"Oh dear, he didn't see us!" exclaimed Professor Zuzubin. "Well, that is because he has no eyes. He's a giant tubeworm—what a lovely creature. You'd like to take a little swim with him, wouldn't you? He's quite friendly," said Zuzubin vaguely. "Which doesn't really

matter. After all, you'll boil alive in the heat from the hydrothermal vent. If you don't drown first, that is."

George sat down next to Annie and put his arm around her. She was shaking. "Don't look anymore," he said. "He's trying to frighten us. Don't let him." But George himself couldn't tear his eyes away from the hideous picture outside the window.

"I see I still don't please you!" said Zuzubin sorrowfully. Once more, the view from the window shifted. This time, all they could see was mile upon mile of ice floes, stretching away from the window for eternity. "Perhaps you don't like to be warm! Let's try a different view. Maybe you are at the South Pole, in the middle of the Antarctic winter." Strong winds buffeted

the window. A group of penguins could be seen, their heads bowed against the fierce gusts of freezing air.

"You see, little children," Zuzubin continued, enjoying his captive audience, "on the other side of that doorway are all the infinite possibilities. Perhaps you have been shrunk down to quantum size so you can find out what it would be like to be a quark!"

"That can't happen," said George. "It isn't possible."

"Oh, really?" said Zuzubin. "You couldn't become confined forever with the three quarks and the myriad quark-antiquark pairs and gluons swarming around inside a proton? The probability of ever escaping would be very small. No one has ever seen a quark outside a hadron, George, and no one will ever see you—"

"No," insisted George. "That's totally bogus and wrong."

"I leave it to you to find out," said Zuzubin smoothly. "Experiments are a fundamental part of science, and I look forward to watching the results of your attempt to prove me incorrect."

"*Shut up!*" shouted Annie. "We have to get out of here!"

"Please," said Zuzubin. "Don't stay a minute longer than you wish. All you have to do is open the door."

"But we can't!" said Annie, sinking onto the sofa. "Can we? If we open the door, we'll probably die . . ."

"Only probably," said Zuzubin comfortingly.

UNCERTAINTY AND SCHRÖDINGER'S CAT

The *quantum* world is the world of atoms and subatomic particles; the *classical* world is the world of people and planets. They seem to be very different places:

C

Classical: We can know both *where* something is and *how fast* it's moving.

. . .

Classical: A ball traveling from A to B takes a definite path. If there is a wall in the way with two holes, then the ball either goes through one hole or the other.

. . .

Classical: We know the ball is going to B, and not to somewhere else.

. . .

Classical: Gentle observations don't affect the motion of the ball.

Q

Quantum: We *can't* know both exactly, and perhaps we know neither—this is *Heisenberg's Uncertainty Principle*.

. . .

Quantum: A particle takes *all* paths from A to B, including paths through different holes— the paths add up to produce a *wavefunction* rippling out from A.

. . .

Quantum: The particle can reach anywhere the wavefunction can reach. We only discover where it is when we make an observation.

. . .

Quantum: Observations completely change the wavefunction—e.g., if we observe our particle at C, the wavefunction *collapses* to be completely at C (then ripples out again).

A Cat in a Box!

But cats (classical!) are made of atoms (quantum!).
Erwin Schrödinger imagined what this might mean
for a cat—though don't do this to your pet cat
(Schrödinger didn't actually do it either)!
He imagined shutting a cat inside a (completely
light- and soundproof) box with some poison,
a radiation detector, and a small amount of
radioactive material. When the detector bleeps
(because an atom produces radiation), then the
poison is automatically released. After a while
in the box, is the cat still alive? The atoms in the
box (including the cat's) take all possible paths:
In some, radiation is produced and the poison
released; but not in others. Only when we make an
observation by opening the box do we discover if
the cat has survived. Before that, the cat is neither
definitely dead nor definitely alive—in a way, it's a
combination of both!

"That means we are trapped . . . ," said George slowly. "In this room . . . forever."

"I have provided plenty of reading material," said Zuzubin. "You'll find all the major texts on the bookshelves, and there is some nourishment in the fridge."

Annie leaped up and went over to the fridge, as though it might show her a way out of this trap. But all it contained was a box of breakfast cereal and five large chocolate bars, with a bottle of milk marked CAT.

"Shredded Wheat and chocolate?" protested Annie.

"A perfectly adequate diet, I have always found," said Zuzubin coldly. "I would have asked you for your culinary preferences, but there really wasn't time. You were in such a terrible hurry."

"This is *your* room, isn't it?" said George, the truth dawning on him. "You live here when you go into hiding—when you disappear, you come here."

"It's peaceful," admitted Zuzubin. "It gives me time to think."

"So there *is* a way out," said George, pointing at Zuzubin through the TV screen. "*You* return to

Foxbridge, so we must be able to. You don't come in here and just take a chance on where you'll end up when you open the door. I bet you've used this room to get to the LHC and to all the other places as well. It's how you travel around."

"Well, yes, of course!" said Zuzubin. "Using the TV remote control, I can make an observation that causes the portal to pick a definite location. So when I open the door, it has taken me to my chosen destination."

"The remote control!" shouted George. "Annie, we must find the remote control for the TV set!"

"Look as hard as you like," sneered Zuzubin. He dangled an object in front of the screen. George slumped in defeat as he realized Zuzubin had the remote in his hand.

"Are you just going to leave us here while my father gets blown up?" said Annie very quietly. It seemed like all hope had gone.

"I am," confirmed Zuzubin. "Would you like to watch? I can play it for you on the television set, if you would like. I am eager to make my guests happy."

"Nooooo!" cried Annie, so loudly and painfully that, back in Foxbridge, Vincent heard her and knew it was time to act.

Chapter Seventeen

Vincent had been hovering behind the old professor, hoping that he would somehow give him a clue how to get Annie and George out of the trap. He knew he could easily overpower the old man, but what good would *that* do? If Zuzubin wouldn't tell him how to extract George and Annie from the bizarre room that he could see on the screen, they could be in even more trouble than before.

Vincent glanced down at George's cell phone, which he'd picked up off the floor, and saw that the screen bore the message: MISSED CALL—HOME. It was at that moment that he heard Annie's cry of pain, and realized he could stand by no longer.

Readying himself, he leaped out from behind the pile of old furniture with a great battle cry. He flew through the air and landed immediately behind Zuzubin, felling him with one swift and totally accurate karate chop. Zuzubin had half turned in surprise, but he toppled like an ancient tree, his eyes rolling back in his head as he crumpled to the floor and lay there, unconscious.

On the screen, Vincent saw Annie and George's astonished faces peering back at him.

"Vincent!" Annie covered the TV screen with kisses.

George dragged her back. "Vincent!" he said. "That was amazing!"

"Vincent, you're the best!" said Annie.

George elbowed her out of the way again. "But, Vince, how are we going to get out?"

"Call my dad!" shouted Annie. "Tell him about the bomb at the LHC!"

Using George's cell phone, Vincent scrolled through and found Eric. He pressed the green phone icon and waited. But all he got was an electronic voice, telling him that the phone was switched off and he would have to try again later.

"The remote control!" shouted George. "Vince, get the remote control from Zuzubin!"

Vincent looked down at the prone figure of Zuzubin, splayed on the floor in his tweed suit, his mustache drooping to one side. He leaned down and pried a remote control out of Zuzubin's fingers, holding it up to the TV screen so George and Annie could see it.

"Is this the one?" said Vincent.

"Yeah!" said George. "That's it! Now can you get us out?"

"Like, er, how?" asked Vincent quietly. "How does this thing work?"

"Oh no," said George. "I didn't think of that. I don't know."

"What if you look at it more closely?" Vincent held the control right next to the screen.

"It's no good," said George in frustration. "The picture isn't clear enough. And Vince," added George, "you've got to be quick. There isn't much time!"

"Call the LHC!" said Annie. "Tell them there's a bomb!"

"Forget it—they wouldn't believe him," said George. "There's only one way—that's to get there and defuse the bomb ourselves."

On the other side, Vincent was staring at the remote control. "When I press 'menu' on my TV remote at home," he said slowly, "it makes the television change between functions. Which is sort of what we need the Inverse Schrödinger Trap to do—we need it to change from a trap to a portal. Shall I try it?" he asked nervously.

"You have to!" said George. "It's our only hope!"

Vincent took a deep breath and pressed the menu button. Nothing happened. He pressed it again and a list came up on Cosmos's screen. The same list of options appeared on the television screen, inside the Schrödinger Trap. He read out loud the first option on the list: "Foxbridge." And then he read out to his friends, waiting inside the Inverse Schrödinger Trap, the second option: "Large Hadron Collider."

"Those must be the locations Zuzubin has visited! If we choose the Collider, perhaps it will take us to the place where he left the bomb! If there are arrow buttons on the remote," said George, speaking very fast, "use them to select LHC."

"I don't know!" fretted Vincent. When it came to dangerous sports like skateboarding and karate, he knew no fear. But faced with sending his friends into certain danger, he felt terrified. "I can't!" he said. "I can't send you to the LHC! We know there's a bomb!"

"Vincent, do it!" said Annie, shoving George out of the way again. "You have to get us to the LHC! If you don't, my dad will never come home—that's what Reeper said! The quicker you do it, the more time we have when we arrive to find the bomb and defuse it. Press the button, Vince! And we'll open the door. Send us there!"

Vincent gave a heart-wrenching sigh and pushed the select button, the cursor hovering over the highlighted "LHC" letters on the screen.

As he did so, George reached forward and pulled open the door . . .

The last Vincent saw of his friends on the television monitor were their backs, disappearing through the portal doorway. Had he managed to work Cosmos correctly? Would they arrive safely at the LHC? Was the LHC, with the bomb primed to go off, a place where he should have sent them? Should he have made them come back to Foxbridge? And what if he'd pressed the wrong button and opened something exotic like a wormhole for them to pass through? What if he'd accidentally sent them back in time? What then?

Vincent gently sank to the floor and waited, his head in his hands, while Zuzubin, the progenitor of all this evil, snored on the floor beside him.

WORMHOLES
AND TIME TRAVEL

Imagine that you are an ant, and you live on the surface of an apple. The apple hangs from the ceiling by a thread so thin that you can't climb up it, so the apple's surface is your entire Universe. You can't go anywhere else. Now imagine that a worm has eaten a hole through the apple, so you can walk from one side of the apple to the other by either of two routes: around the apple's surface (your Universe), or by a short cut, through the wormhole.

Could our Universe be like this apple? Could there be wormholes that link one place in our Universe to another? If so, what would such a wormhole look like to us?

The wormhole would have two mouths, one at each end. One mouth might be at Buckingham Palace in London, and the other on a beach in California. The mouths might be spherical. Looking into the London mouth (a little like looking into a crystal ball), you could see the California beach, with lapping waves and swaying palm trees. Looking into the California mouth, your friend might see you in London, with the palace and its guards behind you. Unlike a crystal ball, the mouths are not solid. You could step right into the big spherical mouth in London, and then after a brief float through a weird sort of tunnel, you would arrive on the beach in California, and could spend the day surfing with your friend. Wouldn't it be wonderful to have such a wormhole?

The apple's interior has three dimensions (east–west, north–south, and up–down), while its surface has only two. The apple's wormhole connects points on the two-dimensional surface by penetrating through the three-dimensional interior. Similarly, your wormhole connects London and California in our three-dimensional Universe by penetrating through a four-dimensional (or maybe even more-dimensional) *hyperspace* that is not part of our Universe.

Our Universe is governed by *laws of physics*. These laws dictate what can happen in our Universe and what cannot. Do these laws permit wormholes to exist? Amazingly, the answer is yes!

Unfortunately (according to those laws) most wormholes will implode—their tunnel walls will collapse—so quickly that nobody and nothing can travel through and survive. To prevent this implosion we must insert into the wormhole a weird form of matter: Matter that has *negative energy*, which produces a sort of anti-gravity force that holds the wormhole open.

Can matter with negative energy exist? Amazingly, again, the answer is yes! And such matter is made daily in physics laboratories, but only in tiny amounts or only for a short moment of time. It is made by borrowing some energy from a region of space that has none, that is by borrowing energy from *the vacuum*. What is borrowed, however, must be returned very quickly when the lender is the vacuum, unless the amount borrowed is very tiny. How do we know? We learn this by scrutinizing the laws of physics closely, using mathematics.

Suppose you are a superb engineer, and you want to hold a wormhole open. Is it possible to assemble enough negative energy inside a wormhole and hold it there long enough to permit your friends to travel through? My best guess is "no," but nobody on Earth knows for sure—yet. We haven't been smart enough to figure it out.

If the laws *do* permit wormholes to be held open, might such wormholes occur naturally in our Universe? Very probably not. They would almost certainly have to be made and held open artificially, by engineers.

How far are human engineers today from being able to make wormholes and hold them open? Very, very far. Wormhole technology, if it is possible at all, may be as difficult for us as spaceflight was for cavemen. But for a very advanced civilization that has mastered wormhole technology, wormholes would be wonderful: the ideal means for interstellar travel!

Imagine you are an engineer in such a civilization. Put one wormhole mouth (one of the crystal-ball-like spheres) into a spaceship and carry it out into the Universe at very high speed and then back to your home planet. The laws of physics tell us that this trip could take a few days as seen and felt and measured in the spaceship, but several years as seen, felt, and measured on the planet. The result is weird: If you now walk into the space-travel mouth, through the tunnel-like wormhole, and out the stay-at-home mouth, you will go back in time by several years. The wormhole has become a machine for traveling backward in time!

With such a machine, you could try to change history: You could go back in time, meet your younger self on a certain day, and tell yourself to stay at home because when you left for work that day, you got hit by a truck.

Stephen Hawking has conjectured that the laws of physics prevent anyone from ever making a time machine, and thereby prevent history from ever being changed. Because the word *chronology*

means "the arrangement of events or dates in the order of their occurrence," this is called the *Chronology Protection Conjecture*. We don't know for sure whether Stephen is right, but we do know two ways in which the laws of physics *might* prevent time machines from being made and thereby protect chronology.

First, the laws might always prevent even the most advanced of engineers from collecting enough negative energy to hold a wormhole open and let us travel through it. Remarkably, Stephen has proved (using the laws of physics) that every time machine requires negative energy, so this would prevent *any* time machine from being made, and not just time machines that use wormholes.

The second way to prevent time machines is this: My physicist colleagues and I have shown that time machines *might* always destroy themselves, perhaps by a gigantic explosion, at the moment when anyone tries to turn them on. The laws of physics give strong hints that this may be so; but we don't yet understand the laws and their predictions well enough to be sure.

So the final verdict is unclear. We do not know for sure whether the laws of physics allow very advanced civilizations to construct wormholes for interstellar travel, or machines for traveling back in time. To find out for certain requires a deeper understanding of the laws than Stephen or I or other scientists have yet achieved.

That is a challenge for you—the next generation of scientists.

Kip

Chapter Eighteen

At TOERAG's secret headquarters, the leaders of the movement also sat glued to a TV screen that gave them a secret insider view of the trigger room at the Large Hadron Collider.

"You will enjoy this," one of the leaders told Reeper, who was pretending he wanted to watch. He dared not show his true feelings in case TOERAG realized he had given away their plans. "Finally you will see Eric Bellis, your old enemy, finished off forever! And best of all, when the Collider is destroyed, the public will think that it exploded because the experiment was too dangerous and that he has lied all along about the risks that it posed."

"Ha ha." Reeper forced a hollow laugh. "How . . . extremely riveting . . ." He'd hoped that his escape into space to meet George on the fast-orbiting asteroid would somehow have foiled this appalling plot.

The clock ticked onward. The meeting at the Collider was scheduled to start at seven thirty. It was already seven fifteen. The trigger room was filling up with scientists. The trigger room in the electronics cavity was a very secret and secure place to hold a meeting. Although it was underground, like the accelerator tunnels and the detector cavities, this part was not sealed off because a very thick wall protected the scientists in the trigger room from the workings of the experiment.

It was also safe and private. Or so the Order of Science to Benefit Humanity believed. Not knowing that someone had deliberately planted a hidden camera, they thought there was no way they could be seen or overheard in this location. As it was, their every word and action was seen elsewhere, by the very same people the Order had such good reason to avoid.

In the middle of the room sat little Cosmos, slightly

the worse for wear after his lengthy interviews with The Grid, his screen smudged and wonky, and several wires sticking out at the back. A scientist walked into the room and inspected him, wincing as he noticed the damage done to the silver laptop.

"Is that Bellis?" said the television evangelist, peering at the screen.

"No," said Reeper. "Bellis is not in the room yet." How he wished he knew for sure that Eric was elsewhere in the Collider, receiving information from George about the quantum mechanical bomb!

"He must get there by seven forty," said another of TOERAG's leaders angrily. "He must be at the nucleus of the explosion."

The minutes ticked by and Reeper held his breath. But just as the clock reached seven thirty, the door to the trigger room flew open and Eric sauntered in, back from his refreshing stroll and determined to meet his fate in fighting form . . .

On the other side of the two-yard-thick wall, George and Annie dashed through the doorway from the Inverse Schrödinger Trap, tripping each other up as they flew through, landing in a tangled heap on a metal floor.

"Get off me!" cried Annie from underneath George. He tumbled to one side and tried to stand up, but his legs felt wobbly. He lay on the floor for a moment, looking at the enormous metal disk that loomed up in front of them.

It was shaped like a very simple drawing of the Sun, round and shiny, with sunbeams radiating out from the central disk. Around the edge of the circle was a ring of blue metal plates, and farther out, huge gray tubular arms stretched forward, as though extending a mighty embrace. The machine towered over them like a cathedral—lofty, silent, and impressive in its sheer bulk. It was the kind of place that made you want to whisper.

George rose unsteadily to his feet. He and Annie seemed to have landed on some kind of platform. She hadn't gotten up yet, but lay scrunched up in a ball on the floor. "Are you okay?" George asked her.

She turned her face up toward him, her eyes still closed. They flickered open for a second, and George saw a flash of brilliant blue; then she squeezed them shut again. "Yeah, I'm fine," she said. "It's like when you've been asleep and someone switches the light on. Just give me a second."

George looked around. "Hello?" he called softly. The noise was lost in the vast empty space, as though the machine had gobbled it up. He could hear a mix of strange repetitive whistling sounds: *PEEooooo—PEEoooooo—PEEooooo*. But there didn't seem to be anyone else around.

What George didn't notice were the tiny motion detectors that had immediately picked up on the unauthorized human arrivals, setting off the alarm system as security cameras transmitted images of him and Annie to security monitors throughout the complex. Down among the intricate machinery, which was carefully blanketed by those thick walls, George and Annie couldn't hear the Klaxons that announced the interlock system had been triggered, initiating a *beam dump*. This meant the proton beams were kicked out of the accelerator's beam pipes and ended up slamming into seven-meter-long graphite cylinders, each contained in a steel cylinder. They had no clue that their presence had been detected and had set off a dramatic and noisy reaction.

Annie staggered to her feet, blinking rapidly. "Are

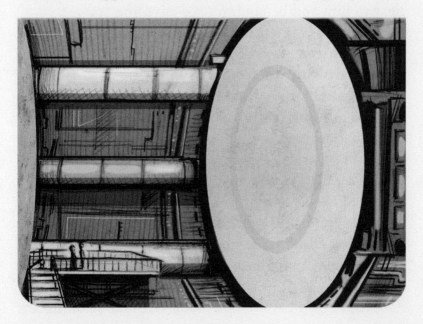

we on a spaceship?" she whispered, looking around. "Is this the engine room of a spacecraft?"

"Don't think so." George shook his head. "It's got normal gravity. And we can breathe without an oxygen tank. I think we're on Earth. This must be the Large Hadron Collider—which means old Cosmos took us to the right place."

"Phew, that's lucky," said Annie, sidling closer to him, as she always did when she was nervous. "But where do we go now? How do we find Dad? And what about—?"

George was just about to reply when, very suddenly, Annie screamed.

"What?" he said, in panic. Annie was standing right next to him and he couldn't see anything scary.

"There's—something—furry—on my leg!" she gasped, frozen with fear. George looked down. The black and white cat from Zuzubin's fiendish trap was winding itself around her ankles.

George gathered the cat up in his arms. "It's okay," he said soothingly to both Annie and the cat. "It's just Zuzubin's kitty. It must have come through the wormhole with us." He scratched the cat, which purred and snuggled closer to him.

"Are you sure it's safe?" said Annie doubtfully, recovering from her fright. "You don't think Zuzubin turned himself into a cat and came with us, to do more evil stuff?"

"Nope, don't think so," said George, stroking the

soft black and white fur. "The cat's friendly now—I think it wanted to get out of that room as much as we did. Look . . ." Under the cat's chin hung an engraved medal. "What does it say?"

Annie twisted the disk around so that she could read it. "*Reward!*" she read. "*Found dead or alive!*" She turned it over. "*Schrödy*—that must be his name. Hold on, it says something else." In smaller letters underneath was written: *I am the cat that walks alone.*

Suddenly the cat hissed and dug his claws into George, who promptly dropped him.

"*Ye-ouch!*" he cried.

"See?" said Annie darkly. "You can't trust anything that came from that horrible room!"

The cat landed on all fours, standing up on his paws like a ballerina *en pointe*. He hissed several times and scratched the metal floor. The fur on his back stood up

and he arched his body, as though confronting an invisible foe. He looked up at George, whiskers quivering, then looked away again.

"What is it, Schrödy?" asked George, squatting down next to him.

"Another trick, I suppose," warned Annie.

Schrödy padded forward a few paces, turned, and came back. He circled George a few times, moved away, and came back once more, all the while casting meaningful glances in George's direction.

"He wants us to follow him," said George slowly.

"You want us to follow a *cat*?" Annie frowned in disbelief.

"I was sent into space by a talking hamster," George pointed out. "And trapped in a weird room by a loony scientist who wants to blow up the LHC. So why not follow a cat? He is Zuzubin's cat, after all."

"I thought he was Schrödinger's cat," threw in Annie.

"Whatever! He's a physics cat—maybe he knows something. Maybe he saw Zuzubin through the window in the Schrödinger Trap, hiding the bomb in the LHC. And"—George looked around the huge almost silent expanse of machinery—"we don't have any other clues to follow right now, or any idea how to find your dad—or the bomb for that matter."

Annie had her phone in her hand but it had no signal.

"If this *is* the Large Hadron Collider," George continued, "which it kinda *has* to be, that means we're underground. That thing"—he pointed at the machine—"is probably some kind of detector, wrapped around the tube where the protons collide."

"Which means we're under the Earth . . . ," said Annie slowly. "Like being in the subway."

"Yup," said George. "We've come out of one trap straight into another. Only this one is a whole lot more dangerous than the last. But we must have arrived here for a reason—Cosmos has brought us to a place at the LHC where Zuzubin has been before. Which must mean the bomb is around here somewhere."

Schrödy hissed again and pawed impatiently at the floor. In the spooky quiet by the great detector, both children imagined they could hear the bomb, ticking down the last few minutes until it exploded, destroying humanity's greatest ever experiment—and a large number of human lives with it.

"So we follow the cat!" Annie broke the silence. "C'mon, Schrödy, show us the way."

Schrödy licked his whiskers and gave them a smug little smile before high-stepping it toward the edge of the platform. A series of blue staircases led downward. At the top of the steps, the cat paused and looked expectantly up at George.

"He wants you to carry him," Annie translated.

"No claws, Schrödy!" George scooped the cat up into his arms and clattered down the stairs. Annie thumped after him, making a ringing noise as she struck

each metal tread on the way down. When they reached the bottom, Schrödy promptly wriggled out of George's arms and landed gracefully on the floor. The kids followed as he stalked along below the curved side of the enormous ATLAS detector.

"George," said Annie, tugging at his sleeve as they tiptoed after the handsome black and white cat. "What if Schrödy isn't showing us the bomb? What then?"

George felt sick to his stomach. "I don't know," he admitted, trying to sound brave. "We'll try and find your dad, and he'll be able to stop it. He *will*, Annie!"

But they both knew they were now deep underground, surrounded by concrete, rock, and layers of metal machinery. If the bomb went off before they could defuse it, there was no way they could escape the blast.

They followed the cat, who led them right to the back of the huge underground chamber. The vast underbelly of ATLAS loomed over them, curving upward, composed of millions of component parts. The kids gazed upward at the largest experiment humanity had ever created.

"If the bomb's in there, we'll never find it," whispered Annie.

George felt despair settle over him . . . but Schrödy had other ideas. Hissing, he flexed his claws once more and dug them into Annie's leg. Even though she was wearing jeans, she still felt it.

"*Oww!* Horrible cat!" she cried.

The cat was unperturbed. He looked up at them both expectantly, waved his long tail, and headed over to a soda machine in the corner. The kids hadn't even noticed it—it was such a familiar object surrounded by so much that was extraordinary that it had melted into the background to become almost invisible.

"Schrödy!" said Annie indignantly. "We're not getting you a drink right now! We have other things to worry about!"

But George was scrutinizing the soda machine. "Annie," he said softly. "Do you notice anything odd about this soda machine?"

She looked at it more closely. The top half was divided into compartments, each with a picture of the drink it would dispense and a button to press to order it. Underneath the different soda options, a handwritten sign was stuck to the front of the machine. It read:

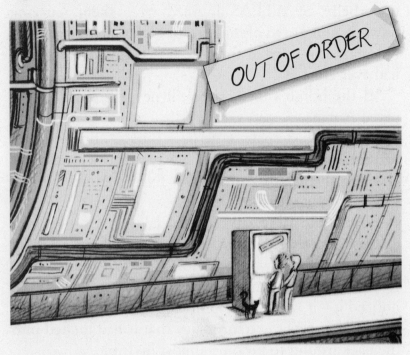

"I've never heard of any of these drinks before," Annie said, turning back to George. "They're not real sodas! I mean, Quark-O-taster! Gloopy Gluon! Nutty Neutrino! What are those? And the lights are on, even though it says 'out of order.'"

George did a quick count. "Eight," he said grimly. "There are eight drink options here. And Reeper said there were eight switches on the bomb."

Annie gasped. "The bomb is inside the soda machine,

isn't it?" she said. "We have to select the right drink to defuse the bomb."

George got out the scrap of paper with the long numerical code that Pooky had kindly excreted for him. "That's it!" he said. "This is the code that makes the switches go live so you can arm—or disarm—the bomb. But the quantum superposition means that all eight switches have been used to arm it, but only one is the important one. But we don't know which one it will be."

"So if we press the wrong button, it will explode?" said Annie.

"Yes," said George. "And there should be no way at all of knowing what the right soda is until we try one, and then it will probably turn out to be the wrong one. But Reeper said he'd done something to the bomb so that you could turn it off after all. He said he'd already made an observation . . ."

"If he made an observation," said Annie, quickly working it out, "that means he must have already looked to see which soda the bomb was going to use so that the quantum superposition thing wouldn't happen. Reeper must have known what switch to use to disarm it. Pooky sent you the code to make the switches go live . . ."

"And we just have to choose the right soda," said George. "That's all."

"That's all . . . ," echoed Annie, staring at the sodas in the machine. She took a step forward.

"Don't touch the machine," George warned her. "We don't know if it's been booby-trapped."

"I won't touch it. But we have to choose . . . Look!" Underneath the slot where you inserted your money was the display that counted up the coins you'd paid for the drink of your choice. The display showed two numbers, which were rapidly counting down—eighty was now replaced by seventy-nine. "I bet that's the number of seconds left until the explosion," said Annie. "So we have to choose something—and fast—or the bomb will go off anyway. What would happen if we pressed all eight switches at once? Would that work?"

"Well, no," said George. "Because it's a soda machine—that's why it's so clever! Think about it—

with a normal soda machine, you can only press one button at a time and get one drink. It will only let you make one choice. So we can't press more than one button now either."

"But which button do we press?" asked Annie.

George gulped and read along the top row of drinks. "*Fizzy-Wi Zzzz,*" he read. "*Quark-O-Taster! Gloopy Gluon. Phrozen Photon. Nutty Neutrino. Electron Energy Drink. Hi-Hi-Hi-GG-Up! Lemon-flavored Iced Tau.*" The figures on the time display were now at sixty, showing that the seconds were dwindling fast. George looked down at Schrödy. "Any ideas?" he asked. The cat seemed to shake his head sadly, as if to say he'd done all he could. He curled up on George's feet and started washing his whiskers. "Annie?" said George hopefully.

"One of them," said Annie, "must be the odd one out . . . One of them must be the setting that Reeper used to make the quantum observation so that the bomb was made to choose one of the eight codes. But which one?"

"W and Z bosons . . . ," George repeated to himself. "Quark . . . Gluon, Photon, Neutrino. Electron, Higgs, and Tau. Which one are you?" Suddenly his brain lit up like the lights on the soda machine. "Eureka!" he cried. "I've got it! It's the Higgs! That's the odd one out."

"Are you sure?" said Annie. The time display now showed they were only thirty seconds away from the explosion.

"Higgs," said George quickly. "It's the only particle that doesn't spin on its axis. The Gluon and Photon have one unit of spin and Neutrino, Electro, and Tau have half a unit."

"Press it!" urged Annie. "Press it, George, *now*! Before it's too late!"

As George leaned forward, the time display showed fifteen seconds left. His hand hovered.

What if he was wrong?

What if he pressed the wrong button and was responsible for blowing up the Large Hadron Collider—and everyone and everything inside it?

A memory nagged at the back of his mind. Eric had once talked about how all observations in quantum theory were fundamentally unpredictable ("indeterminate" had been the word he'd used). Physicists could only calculate the *probability* of a particular result, and only in special situations was the probability a certainty. How, then, had Reeper been able to force the bomb to choose "Hi-Hi-Hi-GG-Up"? He looked down at Pooky's piece of paper—and realized that the last character on the line of symbols was not a number at all, but a capital *H*.

The display was still ticking down—9—8—7—6—5—when George, finally sure that he had worked it out, struck the button to choose the Higgs drink.

Immediately the lights stopped flashing on the <u>front</u> of the machine. Only the Hi-Hi-Hi-GG-Up button continued flashing. The time display froze at four seconds. ENTER CODE scrolled across a window by the drinks button.

George quickly punched in the number part of Pooky's code, upon which the whole machine briefly lit up and trembled. The time display disappeared and the word DISARMED appeared in its place.

As the kids watched in amazement, they heard a clunking noise, and the machine dispensed a can of soda into the transparent tray at the bottom and promptly switched itself off.

"Well!" said George. "That's not at all what I expected!"

Schrödy purred happily, and Annie sank to the floor in relief. Suddenly they heard something else — this time the sound of a heavy door being flung back and footsteps approaching. The footsteps got closer, and a disheveled-looking Eric came round the edge of the great machine and ground to a halt when he saw the kids.

"Annie! George!" cried Eric. "What the blazing stars is going on?" Behind him appeared a phalanx of bemused-looking scientists who had hot-footed it to the ATLAS cavern.

When the alarms had gone off, the scientists had quickly realized that somehow there were two small people in the ATLAS Detector Cavern! Pushing his way through the crowd gathered around the computer screen, which showed the image of the intruders, Eric had realized to his horror that the duo bore a striking resemblance to his daughter Annie and her best friend, George. With the other scientists, he had watched in shock as the two figures had set off down the staircase in front of ATLAS and fallen out of view of the cameras. At that moment, Eric snapped into action and ran from the trigger room, determinedly striking out in the direction of the ATLAS detector.

"Dad!" said Annie, falling on him and hugging him. "You're safe! The LHC isn't going to blow up! Science isn't over!"

"What are you talking about?" exclaimed Eric.

"Professor Bellis," said one of the other scientists. "Can you explain why two children, apparently related to you, have managed to appear in the sealed underground section of the Large Hadron Collider, thus triggering the interlock system and forcing a beam dump?"

"Ah, Doctor Ling," said Eric, nodding at the scientist who had just spoken.

"Could you kindly explain what is going on?" Under Dr. Ling's arm was Cosmos, the little silver laptop. Even in his hurry to follow Eric as he had shot out of the trigger room, headed for the ATLAS detector cavern, Dr. Ling had clearly not wanted to leave Cosmos unguarded.

"Er, well, no!" said Eric, and the scientists began to frown. But George quickly stepped forward.

"Um…hello, everyone," he said. "Sorry about this. There was this quantum mechanical bomb inside the soda machine."

"The soda machine?" said Dr. Ling. "But that's been out

271

of order for ages! No one ever uses it . . . ah," he said. "So that it made it a really clever place to hide a bomb."

"If the bomb had gone off," continued George, "the whole Collider would have been destroyed. We—that is, me and Annie, because I would never have worked it out all by myself—knew there were eight switches that arm or disarm the bomb. There are eight different soda options in the machine, which means each one represents one of the switches on the bomb. We had the code here"—he waved the scrap of paper with Pooky's code on it—"and we knew that the designer of the bomb had, in secret, already made an observation. So we just had to work out which option it was—and that was all about picking the right soda. We thought it must be the 'Higgs,' because all the others are the names of particles that spin on their axis and the Higgs doesn't; but actually"—he looked over at Annie—"it was the right choice because the code here ends in *H*. We picked Higgs, entered the code, and the bomb has now been disarmed."

"Ah . . . the first time the Higgs has definitely been observed at the Large Hadron Collider," said one scientist. "And it was via a soda machine!"

The other scientists whispered among themselves. "A quantum mechanical bomb?" they muttered. "Who could think up such a fiendish device?"

"But how could this awful thing have happened?" said Dr. Ling, sounding anxious. "Who could have wanted to cause such devastation and destruction?"

George and Annie looked at each other. Annie stood up and started to explain this time.

"This organization—TOERAG . . ." The scientists groaned, but Annie carried on: "TOERAG wanted to blow up the Collider while you were all here so that it would appear that the high-energy experiment had gone wrong. They thought that it would kill two birds with one stone—all the world's top physicists would be gone *and* people would think that these kind of experiments were too dangerous and they would never be tried again."

"I don't understand," said Dr. Ling. "How did they manage this? We have maximum security at the Collider. How could they have gotten in?"

"They had an insider," George explained.

"It was Zuzubin, wasn't it?" broke in Eric sorrowfully. "He betrayed us, didn't he? George, do you know why?"

Eric looked so sad that George didn't want to mention Zuzubin's treachery anymore. But he had to answer the question.

"Er, well, Annie and I—we think that Zuzubin wanted to use old Cosmos as a time machine and go back to the past. He wanted to make it look like his theories—the ones that everyone has forgotten about— were right after all. And that you were wrong. He was also trying to show that he predicted the Large Hadron

Collider would explode so that his theories would appear to be correct."

Eric took off his glasses and polished them on his shirttails. "Oh dear," he said. "Poor old Zuzubin."

"What do you mean, *poor old Zuzubin*?" said George hotly. "He tried to blow us all up! You can't feel sorry for him."

"He must have gone crazy," said Eric, shaking his head. "The Zuzubin I knew would never have done anything like this. He would have known that science is an ongoing story. It isn't about who's right or wrong, it's about progression. It's about doing the best work you can and then letting the scientists who come after you build on what you created. It may be that your theories are disproved—that's the risk you take. To try anything new means taking risks and if you don't do that, then you will never achieve anything meaningful. And of course we get it wrong sometimes. That's the point. You have to try and fail and start again, and keep going—not just in science; in life as well."

"Indeed," added Dr. Ling. "The greatest challenges come not when our predictions turn out to be accurate, but when they're not and instead, we discover new information that means we have to change everything we thought we knew."

Just then, Dr. Ling's pager bleeped furiously, as did the pagers of all the other scientists present, making a chirping noise—it sounded as if a flock of starlings had flown into the room. Everyone seized their pager and read the short message. A huge shout went up.

"What is it?" George asked Eric. "What's going on?"

He hugged both children again. "It's ATLAS!" he said. "He's got a result for us! Just when we least expected it! He's got some new information about the early Universe. Now, if I can put that information into Cosmos . . ." He trailed off.

All the scientists fell silent as they remembered that the difficult question of Eric's guardianship of Cosmos had not yet been resolved.

Dr. Ling stood there, looking thoughtful. "Professor Bellis," he said very courteously, "I believe there is a matter that we must deal with before we can investigate this new and exciting piece of information from ATLAS. Before I ask the Order of Science to vote on whether you should remain as the sole custodian of Cosmos, I would like to know—how is it that these two children know so much? How have two mere kids managed to use their unexpected knowledge of quantum theory to prevent an enormous and catastrophic event today at the Large Hadron Collider—an event that would have put back the progress of humanity by centuries?"

Eric didn't get a chance to speak as George interrupted.

"I can tell you that," he answered. "We know stuff because Eric is always explaining things to us. But he doesn't just *tell* us—he gets us to go on journeys with him so that we have to work stuff out for ourselves. He helps us by giving us knowledge, but he also gets us to use our brains to make that knowledge mean something."

"And he uses Cosmos to do this?" queried Dr. Ling.

"Cosmos helps him to make it fun and exciting for us," said George. "That way, we learn things, and then, when we face new challenges, we know how to apply what we learned to different situations and come up with answers. But also"—George shot a worried look at Eric but decided to continue—"we wouldn't have been able to do this—to save all these lives and the Large Hadron Collider—if it hadn't been for Doctor Reeper. He put himself in danger to join TOERAG—who knows what they might have done to him if they had found out he betrayed them? And he sent his avatar into space to tell me about the bomb. Without him, we could never have stopped them. Will you think again about letting him rejoin the Order of Science? He really deserves to be welcomed back."

"Hm," said Dr. Ling. "Very interesting. I will put these matters to a vote. All those in favor of Eric Bellis remaining as the operator of Cosmos, please raise your hands."

A forest of hands went up.

"All those not in favor?"

Not a single arm was raised.

"All those who would like to readmit Graham Reeper to the Order of Science?"

Even with Eric's hand raised, they were still two votes short of a yes.

"George and Annie," said Eric pleasantly, "I believe you are both members of the Order. Would you like to vote?"

They both smiled and raised their hands.

"In that case," said Dr. Ling, handing Cosmos over to Eric, "I would like to return Cosmos to your guardianship once more. And we will find Doctor Reeper and re-award him his fellowship. For saving science from destruction . . ."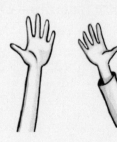

"Thank you," said Eric, clutching Cosmos gratefully. "Thank you,

Doctor Ling. Thank you, colleagues from the Order of Science. But most of all, thank *you*, Annie and George."

"Just one thing," said Dr. Ling as the group started to disperse toward the elevator. "Professor Bellis—no more pigs. Please. Not with the supercomputer, anyway."

"Of course," said Eric hastily. "I'll use my car next time I need to move a pig . . . When I've found him again," he added to himself under his breath. This would be the first item on his to-do list, after he'd examined the results of the experiments into the beginning of the Universe.

"Incidentally," said Dr. Ling as they joined the back of the line for the elevator, "did I see a *cat* in here? I can't believe it—how could a cat get down here?"

"Oh yes, that was Schrödy. He was—" Annie started to say, but then fell silent. Looking around, she saw no sign of the black and white cat. "Perhaps he's gone into another dimension," she speculated in surprise. "After all, he has ten to choose from, if M-Theory is correct."

"Schrödy?" Dr. Ling enquired.

"An imaginary friend," said George firmly. "Of Annie's. She's still very young, sir, and she still has these fantasies— Ouch! Ouch! Annie, get off me . . ."

M–THEORY—ELEVEN DIMENSIONS!

How can we combine Einstein's classical Theory of General Relativity, which describes gravity and the shape of the whole Universe, with the quantum theory explaining tiny fundamental particles and all the other forces?

The most successful attempts all involve *extra space dimensions* and *supersymmetry*.

The extra dimensions are rolled up very tightly so that large objects don't notice them!

Supersymmetry would mean more fundamental particles: e.g., photinos to go with photons, and squarks to go with quarks! (The LHC may see these, and perhaps even detect extra dimensions.)

The theory of *superstrings* (supersymmetric strings) replaces particles (dots) with tiny "strings" (lines). By vibrating in different ways—like different notes on a guitar string—strings behave like different types of particle. Although this sounds strange, strings *can* explain gravity!

Superstrings must exist in ten dimensions—so six extra space dimensions must be hidden away. We don't understand yet exactly how this happens.

In 1995 Ed Witten suggested that the varied types of superstring theories are all different approximations to a *single* theory in *eleven* dimensions, which he called *M-Theory*.

Scientists disagree on what the *M* means: Is it magic, mystery, master, mother, or perhaps membrane? Future generations of physicists will discover the truth!

Scientists have studied M-Theory very hard since then, but still don't know exactly what it is, or if it really is a Theory of Everything.

Chapter Nineteen

Back at ground level, in the control room at CERN, the scientists gathered gleefully around the banks of computer monitors to review the surprising new data uncovered by ATLAS and the high-energy collisions that were taking place in the tunnels below. Dr. Ling and Eric were very busy, inputting these results into Cosmos.

"This is very exciting," Eric said to George and Annie. "This new information from ATLAS will allow us to run a simulation of the Universe backward on Cosmos. We can start at today and work all the way back for thirteen point seven billion years. It's going to be quite a show!"

"Um, Dad . . . ," said Annie. "Before you do that, could you give Mom a call? She was really worried about you. She'll want to know that you're okay."

"Oh, of course!" said Eric, picking up one of the phones on the desk and dialing. "Hello, Susan!" he said into the handset. "Yes, yes, I'm fine . . . What? Annie? Lost? No, she's here with me . . . How did she get to Switzerland? Ah, well, that's a long story . . . No, no, George is here too . . . Yes, we will be back in time for the party . . . No, I haven't forgotten that I promised to pick up the cake . . ."

As Eric struggled to explain how the two kids had shown up safe and sound at the Large Hadron Collider, George tapped Dr. Ling on the shoulder.

"Doctor Ling," he said. "What about TOERAG? What will happen to them now?"

The scientist looked very serious. "I have put out an international alert," he told George. "I hope that they will be found and arrested. They endangered lives with their actions, and if it hadn't been for you and Annie, today would have been a tragedy."

"Will you find them?"

"Wherever they are on this planet, we will track them down."

"TOERAG wasn't trying to protect people at all, was it?" asked George. "They just frightened people into joining them."

"Yes, George," said Dr. Ling. "They pretended they wanted to watch over humanity, but that wasn't true. They used a good motive to hide a bad one—which is a truly evil thing to do."

"My parents don't like science much," confessed George. "They think it damages the planet. They're trying to live a green life."

"Then they are people to whom we, as scientists, should listen. We shouldn't ignore their point of view. The planet belongs to all of us, and we need to be able to work together to make a difference."

George felt quietly proud of his mom and dad.

Meanwhile Annie had grabbed one of the other LHC phones and was talking to Vincent, back in Foxbridge.

"You did *what*?" She burst out laughing. Covering the phone with one hand, she turned to George. "Vincent put Zuzubin into the Inverse Schrödinger Trap! Zuzubin was just coming to when Vincent opened the doorway and pushed him through it!"

George took the phone from Annie. "Wow! That was a cool move," he said admiringly to Vincent. George had to admit he was grateful to Vincent, and that perhaps, just perhaps, he and Vincent might become friends in the future.

On the other end of the line Vincent was laughing. "It was nothing!" he said modestly. "Nothing like what you did, anyway. I just thought it was the safest place to keep him, until Eric gets back. I can see him on the monitor—he's furious! But I've locked the door so he can't open it again."

"Can he escape?" asked George.

"Nope," said Eric, who'd overheard the conversation. "Zuzubin is pretty much stuck there. Until we get back to Foxbridge tomorrow—by airplane, just like normal people. Don't you worry, kids, I'll deal with Zuzubin when we get back. And yes, George, I'll track down Freddy and we'll find him a permanent home too."

Annie took the phone from George. "Bye, Vince!" she said happily. "See you tomorrow! We have to go now—my dad is about to run the Universe backward on Cosmos! We're about to go back to the beginning of everything and see what it was like at the Big Bang!"

Eric sat in front of the supercomputer, pecking away at the keys, Dr. Ling peering intently over his shoulder. Annie and George pushed through the small crowd of scientists who were gathering silently around them so that they could see the screen—columns of numbers were quickly scrolling across it, while in the corner a graph with a little red line was inching across and down, heading toward the bottom of the screen. "That's the diameter of the Universe," Eric said, pointing. "It's shrinking to zero as Cosmos approaches the Big Bang."

As George watched, the line suddenly headed

steeply downward, plunging almost vertically toward the bottom of the graph. "That's inflation," murmured Dr. Ling. "A period of exponential expansion. We are already well into the first second of the Universe's life."

Only the steady noise of computers and air conditioning broke the silence for the next few minutes. George couldn't take his eyes off the little line. It was almost at the bottom of the screen—then seemed to pull up a tiny bit. It was still falling, but not quite so steeply.

George stared—and it did it again. Someone behind

him took a deep breath. George glanced at Eric—and saw that he was beaming in delight, his eyes flicking back and forth over the unceasing columns of numbers.

"Not what we expected!" Eric whispered to himself. "Not what we expected at all!"

"What isn't?" asked Annie.

Her father turned to face her, smiling in delight. "What we've hoped for from the start, Annie. New physics! You see, it seems there isn't one at the Big Bang after all!" He turned back to Cosmos, and started typing rapidly.

Annie turned to George. "There isn't what?" she asked.

George was still watching the graph. The little line was still going down, but had leveled off so much now that it was hugging the bottom of the screen, almost horizontal. "I think I know . . . ," he replied.

Eric sat back with an air of triumph. "You'll see!" he cried, then leaned forward and pressed F4. With that, a small beam of light shot out from Cosmos's screen and sketched the shape of a window, hanging in the air above the heads of the assembled scientists, Dr. Ling and Eric and Annie and George. At first the window looked dark, with a round blurred object hanging in the center of it. But very quickly the blue and green sphere came into sharp focus, and they were looking at planet Earth, turning on its axis as it traveled along its orbit around its parent star, the Sun. Cosmos brought the window closer to the Earth, so that it could be clearly seen, with its familiar patterns of continents and oceans, with the deserts and great forests that cover the surface of this most beautiful and habitable of planets. But even as they watched, the surface of the Earth seemed to be changing shape . . .

TIME: **NOW** 13.7 billion years since the Big Bang

MODERN HUMANS APPEAR.

THE AGE OF THE DINOSAURS COMES TO AN END.

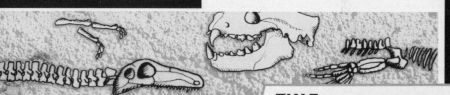

PANGAE—ALL THE EARTH'S CONTINENTS UNITED IN ONE BIG LAND MASS—BREAKS APART.

DINOSAURS BEGIN TO ROAM OUR PLANET.

1 billion
= 1,000
million, or
1,000,000,000

OXYGEN FROM PHOTOSYNTHESIS BEGINS TO
COLLECT IN THE EARTH'S ATMOSPHERE.

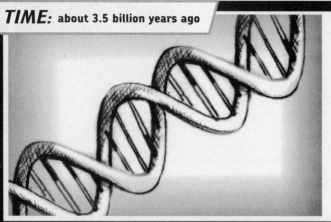

LIFE ON
EARTH BEGINS . . .

THE EARLY EARTH IS A DANGEROUS PLACE . . .

. . . AS IS THE EARLY SOLAR SYSTEM AS THE PLANETS FORM.

OUR SUN IS BORN.

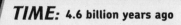

TIME: 4.6 billion years ago

A BEAUTIFUL SPIRAL GALAXY—THE MILKY WAY.

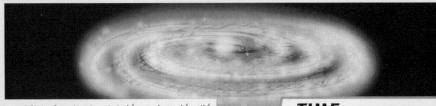

THE FIRST STARS EXPLODE AND BLAST A MIX OF DIFFERENT ATOMS INTO SPACE, WHICH WILL END UP IN THE NEXT GENERATION OF STARS ALL ACROSS THE UNIVERSE.

PATCHES OF GAS COLLAPSE INTO BLOBS THAT HEAT UP SO MUCH THEY RELEASE NUCLEAR ENERGY—TO BECOME THE FIRST STARS.

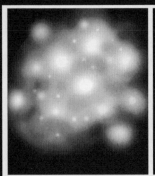

DENSE PATCHES OF DARK MATTER AND GAS ARE ATTRACTED TOGETHER BY GRAVITY.

THE COSMIC DARK AGES LAST A FEW HUNDRED MILLION YEARS.

THE FOG LIFTS AS THE FIRST WHOLE ATOMS APPEAR—THE COSMIC MICROWAVE BACKGROUND RADIATION IS NOW FREE TO TRAVEL ACROSS THE UNIVERSE.

HOT FOG FILLS THE
UNIVERSE AS THE FIRST
NUCLEI FORM.

TIME: 1 microsecond after the Big Bang

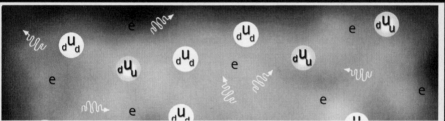

THE QUARK-GLUON PLASMA HAS COOLED, ALLOWING PROTONS AND NEUTRONS TO FORM. MATTER
AND ANTIMATTER ANNIHILATE, RELEASING PHOTONS (PARTICLES OF LIGHT), WHICH CAN'T TRAVEL
FAR THROUGH THE FOGLIKE PLASMA.

TIME: 1 millionth of a
microsecond after the Big Bang

TIME: 10 billionths of a billionth
of a billionth of a microsecond
after the Big Bang

ALL PARTICLES HAVE ACQUIRED MASS WITH
HELP FROM THE HIGGS FIELD.

THE UNIVERSE HAS JUST STOPPED
INFLATING AND RELEASED A LARGE AMOUNT
OF ENERGY. THE UNIVERSE IS FILLED WITH A
QUARK-GLUON PLASMA.

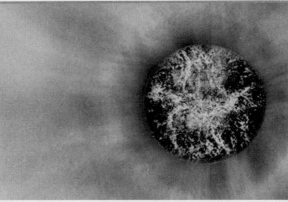

THE UNIVERSE IS SHRINKING VERY FAST AS WE APPROACH THE BIG BANG!

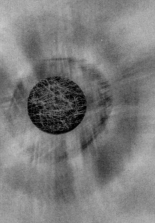

THE REALM OF EXOTIC MATTER AND M-THEORY. STILL SHRINKING BUT NOT QUITE SO FAST . . .

THIS IS WHEN SPACE AND TIME—AS WE UNDERSTAND IT—SHOULD
BEGIN. BUT THE UNIVERSE IS STILL HERE, INCREDIBLY SMALL AND
STILL SHRINKING. PERHAPS IT WILL NEVER REACH A SINGULARITY
AFTER ALL. . . .

Acknowledgments

A book like *George and the Big Bang* doesn't just appear out of nowhere. Many people are involved in making it happen. Working on the whole George series—and in particular, this third volume—has been a pleasure and a privilege. We would like to thank the team at Simon & Schuster for their dedication to publishing the George trilogy in the United States. We would especially like to say a huge thank-you to David Gale, who championed George from the very first and has seen the series through to this final adventure. We'd also like to thank very warmly Navah Wolfe, Dorothy Gribbin, Krista Vossen, Michelle Kratz, and Paul Crichton for their kindness, commitment, and professional expertise.

Gary Parsons has brought George and his friends and foes to life—this time, taking on the challenge of illustrating the Universe backward. And our distinguished researcher Stuart Rankin did a terrific and inventive job. Stuart's contribution incudes the genius of the IST, the essay on the Big Bang, and the deceptively simple explanations of quantum theory and other bizarre and fabulous phenomena. Very dedicated thanks go to Markus Poessel at the Max Planck Institute for his excellent input into the final version of the text.

Once more a roll call of very eminent scientists came forward to explain their work to a young audience. Our thanks go to Paul Davies, Michael S. Turner, Lawrence Krauss, and Kip S. Thorne for their brilliant contributions. We'd also like to thank Roger Weiss at NASA for his photographic insights into the wonders of the Universe and all our friends at NASA for the use of the cosmic images.

And, most of all, we would like to thank our young readers for wanting another George book! Good luck on all your cosmic journeys!

Lucy Hawking